Sarah.

A very Happy Birthday,

love as always

Mum & Mike

'Aug 2000

x x x

Ben, in the World

By the same author

DORIS LESSING

Ben, in the World

the sequel to
The Fifth Child

Flamingo
An Imprint of HarperCollins*Publishers*

Flamingo
An Imprint of HarperCollins*Publishers*
77–85 Fulham Palace Road,
Hammersmith, London w6 8jb

www.**fire**and**water**.com

Flamingo is a registered trademark of
HarperCollins*Publishers* Limited

Published by Flamingo 2000
1 3 5 7 9 8 6 4 2

A catalogue record for this book
is available from the British Library

ISBN 0 00 226195 2

Typeset in Bembo by
Rowland Phototypesetting Ltd,
Bury St Edmunds, Suffolk

Printed and bound in Great Britain by
Clays Ltd, St Ives plc

Author's Notes

'The Cages' were described to me in miserable detail ten years ago by someone who had seen them in a research institute in London. Here they are set in Brazil, because of the exigencies of the plot, but I am sure no such unpleasant phenomenon exists in Brazil.

The authorities have cleared the gangs of criminal children from the streets of the centre of Rio. They are no longer permitted to annoy tourists.

Acknowledgements

My grateful thanks, as always, to my agent Jonathan Clowes, and in particular for the contributions he has made to this story of Ben Lovatt, the Fifth Child.

And my gratitude too to Suzette Macedo for her advice on the Brazilian part of the book; and to Martin Copertari who helped me with information about conditions in north-west Argentina, a splendidly beautiful part of the world.

'How old are you?'

'Eighteen.'

This reply did not come at once because Ben was afraid of what he knew was going to happen now, which was that the young man behind the glass protecting him from the public set down his biro on the form he was filling in, and then, with a look on his face that Ben knew only too well, inspected his client. He was allowing himself amusement that was impatient, but it was not quite derision. He was seeing a short, stout, or at least heavily built man – he was wearing a jacket too big for him – who must be at least forty. And that face! It was a broad face, with strongly delineated features, a mouth stretched in a grin – what did he think was so bloody funny? – a broad nose with flaring nostrils, eyes that were greenish, with sandy lashes, under bristly sandy brows. He had a short neat pointed beard that didn't fit with the face. His hair was yellow and seemed – like his grin – to shock and annoy, long, and falling forward in a slope, and in stiff locks on either side, as if trying to caricature a fashionable cut. To cap it all, he was using a posh voice; was he taking the mickey? The clerk was going in for this minute inspection because he was discommoded by Ben to the point of feeling angry. He sounded peevish when he said, 'You can't be eighteen. Come on, what's your real age?'

Ben was silent. He was on the alert, every little bit of him, knowing there was danger. He wished he had not come to this place, which could close its walls around him. He was listening to the noises from outside, for reassurance from his normality. Some pigeons were conversing in a plane tree on the pavement, and he was with them, thinking how they sat gripping twigs with pink claws that he could feel tightening around his own finger; they were contented, with the sun on their backs. Inside here, were sounds that he could not understand until he had isolated each one. Meanwhile the young man in front of him was waiting, his hand holding the biro and fiddling it between his fingers. A telephone rang just beside him. On either side of him were several young men and women with that glass in front of them. Some used instruments that clicked and chattered, some stared at screens where words appeared and went. Each of these noisy machines Ben knew was probably hostile to him. Now he moved slightly to one side, to get rid of the reflections on the glass that were bothering him, and preventing him from properly seeing this person who was angry with him.

'Yes. I am eighteen,' he said.

He knew he was. When he had gone to find his mother, three winters ago – he did not stay because his hated brother Paul had come in – she had written in large words on a piece of card:

Your name is Ben Lovatt.

Your mother's name is Harriet Lovatt.

Your father's name is David Lovatt.

You have four brothers and sisters, Luke, Helen, Jane, and Paul. They are older than you.

You are fifteen years old.

On the other side of the card had been:

You were born ....
Your home address is ....

This card had afflicted Ben with such a despair of rage that he took it from his mother, and ran out of the house. He scribbled over the name *Paul*, first. Then, the other siblings. Then, the card falling to the floor and picked up showing the reverse side, he scribbled with his black biro over all the words there, leaving only a wild mess of lines.

That number, fifteen, kept coming up in questions that were always − so he felt − being put to him. 'How old are you?' Knowing it was so important, he remembered it, and when the year turned around at Christmas, which no one could miss, he added a year. Now I am sixteen. Now I am seventeen. Now, because a third winter has gone, I am eighteen.

'OK, then, when were you born?'

With every day since he had scribbled with that angry black pen all over the back of the card he had understood better what a mistake he had made. And he had destroyed the whole card, in a culminating fit of rage, because now it was useless. He knew his name. He knew 'Harriet' and 'David' and did not care about his brothers and sisters who wished he was dead.

He did not remember when he was born.

Listening, as he did, to every sound, he heard how the noises in that office were suddenly louder, because in a line of people waiting outside one of the glass panels, a woman had begun shouting at the clerk who was interviewing her, and because of this anger released into the air, all the lines began moving and shuffling, and other people were muttering, and then said aloud, like a barking, short angry words like Bastards, Shits – and these were words that Ben knew very well, and he was afraid of them. He felt the cold of fear moving down from the back of his neck to his spine.

The man behind him was impatient, and said, 'I haven't got all day if you have.'

'When were you born? What date?'

'I don't know,' said Ben.

And now the clerk put an end to it, postponing the problem, with, 'Go and find your birth certificate. Go to the Records Office. That'll settle it. You don't know your last employer. You don't have an address. You don't know your date of birth.'

With these words his eyes left Ben's face, and he nodded at the man behind to come forward, displacing Ben, who went straight out of that office, feeling as if all the hairs of his body, the hairs on his head, were standing straight up, he was so trapped and afraid. Outside was a pavement, with people, a little street, full of cars, and under the plane tree where the pigeons were moving about, cooing and complacent, a bench. He sat on it at the other end from a young woman who gave him a glance, but then another, frowned, and went off, looking back at him with *that* look on her face which Ben knew and expected. She was not afraid of him, but thought that she might be soon. Her body was all haste and apprehension, like one escaping. She went into a shop, glancing back.

Ben was hungry. He had no money. There were some broken crusts on the ground, left for the pigeons. He gathered them up hastily, looking about him: he had been scolded for this before. Now an old man came to sit on the bench, and he gave Ben a long stare, but decided not to bother with what his instincts were telling him. He closed his eyes. The sun made a tiny bloom of sweat on the old face. Ben sat on, thinking how he must go back to the old woman, but she would be disappointed in him. She had told him to come to this office and claim unemployment benefit. The thought of her made him smile – a very different grin from the one that had annoyed the clerk. He sat smiling, a small smile that showed a gleam of teeth in his beard, and watched how the old man woke up, to wipe away the sweat that was running down his face, saying to the sweat, 'What? What's that?' as if it had reminded him of something. And then, to cover himself, he said sharply to Ben, 'What do you think you're laughing at?'

Ben left the bench and the shade of the tree and the companionship of the pigeons, and walked through streets knowing he was going the right way, for about two miles. Now he was nearing a group of big blocks of flats. He went direct to one of them, and inside it, saw the lift come running down towards him, hissing and bumping, tried to make himself enter it, but his fear of lifts took him to the stairs. One, two, three . . . eleven flights of grey cold stairs, listening to the lift grumble and crash on the other side of a wall. On the landing were four doors. He went straight to one from where a rich meaty smell was coming, making his mouth fill with water. He turned the door knob, rattled it, and stood back to stare expectantly at the door, which opened. And there an old woman stood, smiling. 'Oh, Ben, there you are,' she said, and put her arm around him to pull him into the room.

Inside he stood slightly crouched, darting looks everywhere, first of all to a large tabby cat that sat on a chair arm. Its fur was standing on end. The old woman went to it, and said, 'There, there, it's all right, puss,' and under her calming hand its terror abated, and it became a small neat cat. Now the old woman went to Ben, with the same words, 'There, Ben, it's all right, come and sit down.' Ben allowed his eyes to leave puss, but did not lose his wariness, sending glances in her direction.

This room was where the old woman had her life. On a gas stove was a saucepan of meat stew, and it was this that Ben had smelled on the landing. 'It's all right, Ben,' she said again, and ladled stew into two bowls, put hunks of bread beside one, for Ben, set her own opposite him, and then spooned out a portion into a saucer for the cat, which she put on the floor by the chair. But the cat wasn't taking any chances: it sat quiet, its eyes fixed on Ben.

Ben sat down, and his hands were already about to dig into the mound of meat, when he saw the old woman shake her head at him. He picked up a spoon and used it, conscious of every movement, being careful, eating tidily, though it was evident he was very hungry. The old woman ate a little, but mostly watched him, and when he had finished, she scraped out from the saucepan everything that was left of the stew, and put it on his plate.

'I wasn't expecting you,' she said, meaning that she would have made more. 'Fill up on bread.'

Ben finished the stew, and then the bread. There was nothing else to eat except some cake, which she pushed towards him, but he ignored it.

Now his attention was free, and she said, slowly, carefully, as if to a child, 'Ben, did you go to the office?' She had told him how to get there.

'Yes.'

'What happened?'

'They said, "How old are you?"'

Here the old woman sighed, and put her hand to her face, rubbing it around there, as if wiping away difficult thoughts. She knew Ben was eighteen: he kept saying so. She believed him. It was the one fact he kept repeating. But she knew that was no eighteen-year-old, sitting there in front of her, and she had decided not to go on with the thoughts of what that meant. *It's not my business – what he really is*, sums up what she felt. *Deep waters! Trouble! Keep out!*

He sat there like a dog expecting a rebuke, his teeth revealed in that other grin, which she knew and understood now, a stretched, teeth-showing grin that meant fear.

'Ben, you must go back to your mother and ask her for your birth certificate. She'll have it, I'm sure. It'd save you all the complications and the questions. You do remember how to get there?'

'Yes, I know that.'

'Well, I think you should go soon. Perhaps tomorrow?'

Ben's eyes did not leave her face, taking in every little move-ment of eyes, mouth, her smile, her insistence. It was not the first time she had told him to go home to find his mother. He did not want to. But if *she* said he must . . . For him what was difficult was this: here there was friendship for him, warmth, kindness, and here, too, insistence that he must expose himself to pain and confusion, and danger. Ben's eyes did not leave that face, that smiling face, for him at this moment the bewildering face of the world.

'You see, Ben, I have to live on my pension. I have only so much money to live on. I want to help you. But if you got some money – that office would give you money – and that would help me. Do you understand, Ben?' Yes, he did. He knew money. He had learned that hard lesson. Without money you did not eat.

And now, as if it was no great thing she wanted him to do, just a little thing, she said, 'Good, then that is settled.'

She got up. 'Look, I've got something I think would be just right for you.'

Folded over a chair was a jacket, which she had found in a charity shop, searching until there was one with wide shoulders. The jacket Ben had on was dirty, and torn, too.

He took it off. The jacket she had found fitted his big shoulders and chest but was loose around the waist. 'Look, you can pull it in.' There was a belt, which she adjusted. And there were trousers, too. 'And now I want you to have a bath, Ben.'

He took off the new jacket and his trousers, obedient, watching her all the time.

'I'm going to put away these trousers, Ben.' She did so. 'And I have got new underpants, and vests.'

He was standing naked there, watching, while she went next door to a little bathroom. His nostrils flared, taking in the smell of water. Waiting, he checked all the smells in the room, the fading aromas of the good stew, a warm friendly smell; the bread, which smelled like a person; then a rank wild smell – the cat, still watching him; the smell of a slept-in bed, where the covers had been pulled up covering the pillows, which had a different smell.

8

And he listened, too. The lift was silent, behind two walls. There was a rumbling in the sky, but he knew aeroplanes, was not afraid of them. The traffic down there he did not hear at all – he had shut it out of his awareness.

The old woman came back, and said, 'Now, Ben.' He followed her, clambered into the water, and crouched in it. 'Do sit down,' she said. He hated the submission to the dangerous slipperiness, but now he was sitting in hot water to his waist. He shut his eyes, and with his teeth bared, this time in a grin of resignation, he let her wash him. He knew this washing was something he had to do, from time to time. It was expected of him. In fact he was beginning to enjoy water.

Now the old woman, Ben's eyes no longer fastened on her face, allowed herself to show the curiosity she felt, which could never be assuaged – or indulged in.

Under her hands was a strong broad back, with fringes of brown hair on either side of the backbone, and on the shoulders a mat of wet fur: it felt like that, as if she were washing a dog. On the upper arms there was hair, but not so much, not more than could be on an ordinary man. His chest was hairy, but it wasn't like fur, it was a man's chest. She handed him the soap but he let it slide into the water, and dug around furiously for it. She found it, and lathered him vigorously, and then used a little hand-shower to get it all off. He bounded out of the bath, and she made him go back, and she washed his thighs, his backside, and then, his genitals. He had no self-consciousness about these, and so she didn't either. And then, he could get out, which he did laughing, and shaking himself into the towel she held. She enjoyed hearing him laugh: it was like a bark. Long ago she had a dog who barked like that.

She dried him, all over, and then led him back to the other room, naked, and made him put on his new underpants, his new vest, a charity shop shirt, his trousers. Then she put a towel around his shoulders and as he began to jerk about in protest, she said, 'Yes, Ben, you have to.'

She trimmed his beard first. It was stiff and bristly, but she was able to make a good job of it. And now his hair, and that was a different matter, for it was coarse and thick. The trouble was his double crown which, if cut short, showed like stubbly whorls on the scalp. It was necessity that had left the hair on the top of his head long, and at the sides. She told him that one of these new clever hairdressers would make him look like a film star, but since he did not take this in, she amended it to, 'They could make you look so smart, Ben, you'd not know yourself.'

But he didn't look too bad now, and he smelled clean.

It was early evening and she did what she would have done alone: she brought out cans of beer from her fridge, filled her glass, and then she filled one for him. They were going to spend the evening doing what he liked best, watching television.

First she found a piece of paper and wrote on it:

Mrs Ellen Biggs
11 Mimosa House
Halley Street, London SE6.

She said, 'Ask your mother for your birth certificate. If she has to send for it, then tell her she can always write to you care of me – and here is the address.'

He did not answer: he was frowning.

'Do you understand, Ben?'

'Yes.'

She did not know whether he did or not, but thought so.

He was looking at the television. She got up, switched it on, and came back by way of the cat. 'There, there puss, it's all right.' But the cat never for one moment took its eyes off Ben.

And now it was an easy pleasant evening. He did not seem to mind what he saw. Sometimes she switched to another channel, thinking he was bored. He did like wildlife programmes, but there wasn't one tonight. This was a good thing, really, because he sometimes got too excited: she knew wild instincts had been aroused. She had understood from the start that he was controlling instincts she could only guess at. Poor Ben – she knew he was that, but not how, or why.

At bedtime she unrolled on to the floor the futon he slept on, and put blankets beside it in case: he usually did not use coverings. The cat, seeing that this enemy was on the floor, leaped up on to the bed and lay close against the old woman's side. From there she could not watch Ben, but it was all right, she felt safe. When the lights were off the room was not really dark, because there was a moon that night.

The old woman listened for Ben's breathing to change into what she called his night breathing. It was, she thought, like listening to a story, events or adventures that possibly the cat would understand. In his sleep Ben ran from enemies, hunted, fought. She knew he was not human: 'not one of us' as she put it. Perhaps he was a kind of yeti. When she had seen him first, in a supermarket, he was prowling – there was only that word for it – as he reached out to grab up loaves of bread. She had had a glimpse of him then, the wild man, and she had never forgotten it. He was a controlled explosion of furious needs, hungers and frustrations, and she knew that even as she said to the attendant, 'It's all right, he is with me.' She handed him a pie she had just bought for her lunch, and he was eating it as she led him out of the place. She took him home, and fed him. She washed him, though he had protested that first time. She saw how he reacted to some cold meat – quite alarming it was; but she bought extra meat for him. It was just here where he was most different; meat, he could not get enough. And she was an old woman, eating a little bit of this here, a snack there – an apple, cheese, cake, a sandwich. The stew that day had been just luck: she ate that kind of meal so seldom.

One night, when the three of them had gone to bed, and to sleep, she had woken because of a pressure along her legs. Ben had crept up and laid himself down, his head near her feet, his legs bent. It was the cat's distress that had woken her. But Ben was asleep. It was how a dog lays itself down, close, for company, and her heart ached, knowing his loneliness. In the morning he woke embarrassed. He seemed to think he had done wrong, but she said, 'It's all right, Ben. There's plenty of room.' It was a big bed, the one she had had when she was married.

She thought that he was like an intelligent dog, always trying to anticipate wants and commands. Not like a cat at all: that was a different kind of sensitivity. And he was not like a monkey, for he was slow and heavy. Not like anything she had known. He was Ben, he was himself – whatever that was. She was pleased he was going to find his family. He was hardly communicative, but she had gathered it was a well-off family. And there was his accent which was not what you'd expect, from how he looked. He

seemed to like his mother. If she herself could be good to Ben –
so Ellen Biggs saw it – then his family could too. But if it didn't
work, and he turned up here again, then she would go with him
to the Public Records Office and find out about his age. She was
so confused about this she had given up trying to puzzle it out.
He repeated that he was eighteen, and she had to believe him.
In many ways he was childish, and yet when she took a good
look at that face she could even think him middle-aged, with
those lines around his eyes. Little ones, but still: no eighteen-year-
old could have them. She had actually gone so far in her thoughts
to wonder if the people he belonged to, whoever they were,
matured early, in which case they would die young, according
to our ideas. Middle-aged at twenty, and old at forty, whereas
she, Ellen Biggs, was eighty and only just beginning to feel her
age to the point that she hoped she would not have to make that
annoying journey to the Records Office, and then stand in a
line: the thought made her tired and cross. She fell asleep, listening to Ben dream, and woke to find him gone. The paper
with her address had gone, and the ten-pound note she had left
for him. Although she had expected it, now she had to sit
down, her hand pressing on a troubled heart. Since he had come
into her life, weeks ago, foreboding had come too. Sitting alone
when he had gone off somewhere she was thinking, Where's Ben?
What is he doing? Was he being cheated again? Far too often
had she heard from him, 'They took my money,' – 'They stole
everything.' The trouble was, information came out of him in a
jumble.

'When was that, Ben?'

'It was summer.'

'No, I mean, what year?'

'I don't know. It was after the farm.'

'And when was that?'

'I was there two winters.'

She knew he was about fourteen when he left his family. So what had he been doing for four years?

His mother had been wrong, thinking he had gone right away. He and his gang of truants from school were camping in an empty house on the edge of their town, and from there made forays, shoplifting, breaking into shops at night, and at weekends went to nearby towns to hang about the streets with the local youths, hoping for a fight and some fun. Ben was their leader because he was so strong, and stood up for them. So they thought, but really the reason was that inwardly he was mature, he was a grown man, more of a parent, whereas they were still children. One by one they were caught, sent to borstal, or returned to parents and school. One evening he was standing on the edge of a crowd of fighting youngsters – he did not fight, he was afraid of his strength, his rage – and he realised he was alone, without companions. For a while he was one of a gang of much older youths, but he did not dominate them as he had the young ones. They forced him to steal for them, made fun of him, jeered at his posh accent. He left them and drifted down to the West Country where he fell in with a motorbike gang, which was engaged in warfare with a rival gang. He longed to drive a motorcycle, but could not get the hang of it. But it was enough to be near them, these machines, he loved them so. The gang used him to guard their bikes when they went into a caff, or a pub. They gave him food, and even a little money sometimes. One night the rival gang found him standing over half a dozen machines, beat him up, twelve to one, and left him bleeding. His own gang returned to find a couple of their machines gone, and were ready to beat him up again but found this apparently slow stupid oaf transformed into a whirling screaming fighting madman. He nearly killed one of them. Setting on him all together they subdued him, no bones broken, but again, he was bleeding and sick. He was taken into a pub by a girl who worked there. She washed him down, sat him in a corner, gave him something to eat, talked him into sense again. He was quiet at last, dazed perhaps.

A man came to him, sat down, and asked if he was looking for work. This was how Ben found himself on the farm. He went with Matthew Grindly because he knew that from now on any member of the two gangs seeing him would summon his mates, and he would be beaten up again.

The farm was well away from any main road, down an over-grown and muddy lane. It was neglected, and so was the house, which was large, and bits of it were shut off where the roof leaked too badly. This farm had been left twenty years before by their father to Mary Grindly, Matthew Grindly, and Ted Grindly. A farm, but no money. They were pretty well self-sufficient, living off their animals, fruit trees, the vegetable garden. What fields there were – one after another they had been sold off to neigh-bouring farmers – grew fodder. Once a month, Mary and Matthew – now Mary and Ben – walked into the village three miles off to buy groceries, and liquor for Ted. They walked because their car was rusting in a yard.

When money was needed for food, electricity, rates, Mary said to Matthew, 'Take that beast to market and get what you can for it.' But bills were ignored for months at a time, and often not paid at all.

This disgraceful place tended to be forgotten by everyone: the locals were part ashamed because of it, and part sorry for the Grindlys. It was known that 'the boys' – but they were getting old now – were not far off feeble-minded. They were illiterate, too. Mary had expected to marry, but it had come to nothing. It was she who ran the farm. She told her brothers what to do: mend that fence . . . clean out that byre . . . take the sheep for shearing . . . plant the vegetables. She was at them all day and bitter because she had to be. Then it was Matthew who was doing all the work: Ted was drinking himself to death quietly in his room. He was no trouble, but he couldn't work. Matthew was getting arthritic, and he had chest problems, and soon the hard work was beyond him too. He fed the chickens and looked after the vegetables, but that was about it.

Ben was given a room, with poor furniture in it – very different from the pleasant rooms he had been brought up in. He could eat as much as he wanted. He worked from daylight to dark, every day. He did know that he did most of the work, but not that without him the farm would collapse. This farm, or anything like it, would soon become impossible, when the European Commission issued its diktats, and its spy-eyes circled for ever overhead. The place was a scandal, and a waste of good land. People came tramping along the lane and through the farmyard, hoping to buy it – the telephone had been cut off, for non-payment – and they would be met by Mary, an angry old woman, who told them to go away, and slammed the door in their face.

When on the neighbouring farms they were asked about the

Grindlys, people tended to equivocate, siding with them against officialdom and the curious. If they lost the farm, what would happen to those poor derelicts, Ted and Matthew? They would find themselves in a Home, that's what. And Mary? No, let the poor things live out their time. And they had that chap there who'd come from somewhere, no one knew where, a kind of yeti he looked like, but he did the work well enough.

Once, when Ben had gone with Mary to the village to carry groceries back, he was stopped by a man who said to him, 'You're with the Grindlys, they say. Are they doing right by you?'

'What do you want?' asked Ben.

'What are they paying you? Not much if I know the Grindlys. I'll make it worth your while to come to me. I'm Tom Wandsworth . . .' – he repeated the name, and then again, '. . . and anyone around here will tell you how to get to my farm. Think about it.'

'What did he say?' Mary asked, and Ben told her.

Ben had never been given a pay-book, and terms and conditions of work had not been mentioned. Mary had given him a couple of quid when they went to the village so he could buy toothpaste, that kind of thing. She was impressed that he cared about his personal cleanliness, and liked his clothes neat.

Now she said, 'I'm keeping your wages for you, Ben. You know that.'

How could he know? This was the first time he had heard about it. Mary believed that he was stupid, like her brothers, but now saw trouble loom.

'You don't want to leave us, Ben,' she said. 'You'd not do

better with anyone else. I've got a good little bit of money put aside for you. You can have it any time.'

She pointed to a high-up drawer in her room. Then she fetched a chair, made him stand on it, and held the back steady. There were rolls of notes in the drawer. To Ben it seemed more money than he had imagined possible.

'Is that mine?' he asked.

'Half of it is yours,' said Mary.

And when he had gone out of the room, she hid it somewhere else.

It was Mary he did not want to leave, though he was fond of the cow and enjoyed the antics of the pigs. He thought Mary was good to him. She mended his clothes, bought him a new thick jersey for the winter, and gave him plenty of meat to eat. She was never cross with him, as she was with her brothers.

He had a life the others did not guess at. They all went to bed early, with nothing to occupy their minds, and no television: Ted was usually drunk and snoring by nine or ten, and Mary listened to the news on the radio, and went to her room afterwards. Ben slid out over the sill of his window when the house was quiet, and went about the fields and woods, alone and free – himself. He would catch and eat little animals, or a bird. He crouched behind a bush for hours to watch fox cubs playing. He sat with his back against a tree trunk and listened to the owls. Or he stood by the cow with his arm around her neck, nuzzling his face into her; and the warmth that came into him from her, and the hot sweet blasts of her breath on his arms and legs when she turned her head to sniff at him meant the safety of kindness. Or he stood leaning on a fence post staring up at the night sky, and on clear nights he sang a little grunting song to the stars, or he danced around, lifting his feet and stamping. Once old Mary thought she heard a noise that needed investigation, went to a window, and caught a glimpse of Ben, and crept down in the dark to watch and listen. It really did make her scalp prickle and her flesh go cold. But why should she care what he did for fun? Without him the animals would be unfed, the cows would stay unmilked, the pigs would have to live in their dirt. Mary Grindly was curious about Ben, but not much. She had had too much trouble in her life to care about other people. Ben's coming to the farm she saw as God's kindness to her.

Then Ted fell down some steps when drunk, and died. Surely Matthew should have been next, the half-crippled coughing man, but it was Mary who had a heart attack. Officials of all kinds suddenly became curious, and one of them, demanding to see accounts, asked Ben questions about himself. Ben was going to say something about the money owed to him, but his instincts shouted at him, *Danger* – and he ran away.

He picked apples on a cider farm, and then he picked raspberries. The other pickers were Poles, mostly students, flown in by a contractor of labour, jolly young people determined to have a good time in spite of the long hours they had to work. Ben was silent and watchful, on his guard. There were caravans to sleep in, but he hated that closeness, and the bad air, and when he had finished eating with them, at night, listening to their songs and their jokes and their laughter, he took a sleeping bag into a wood.

When the picking was finished he had a good bit of money, and he was happy, because he knew that it was having no money that made him helpless. One of the singing and joking young people stole his money from his jacket that was hanging above him on a bush where he lay asleep. Ben made himself go back to the farm, thinking of all that money in the drawer, and half of it belonging to him, but the house was locked, the animals were gone, and there were already nettles growing close up around the house. He did not care about Matthew, who had scarcely spoken to him except for unkind remarks such as when the old dog died – 'We don't need another dog, we've got Ben.'

He went home to find his mother but she had moved again. He had to use his wits to find where she was. A house, but nothing like the one he thought of as home. He could not make himself go in, because he saw Paul there, and the rage that was his enemy nearly overcame him.

So he took the old, old road to London, rich London, where surely there must be a little something for him too. There he did find work, was cheated again, lost heart, and Ellen Briggs found him starving in a supermarket.

On the dark pavement outside Mimosa House there seemed to be no one about, but Ben knew how at night a shadow could lengthen and become an enemy, and, turning a corner, he nearly ran into a drunk who was lurching about and swearing and muttering. Ben swerved past and ran across empty streets, not bothering about lights. Not until he reached Richmond did he begin using the crossings, telling himself, *Go* on green, *Stop* on red. There were people about now, quite a lot. On he went, following instincts that worked well if he didn't confuse them with maps and directions, and then he was in a high street and he was hungry. He went into a café that said 'Breakfast All Day', and, as always in a new place, looked hard at faces for that surprised stare that might turn out to be dangerous. But it was too early for people to be noticing much. He was careful to eat his breakfast slowly and attentively, and left the café feeling pleased with himself. Off he went again, and by midday was crossing fields with the sun spreading warmth everywhere. Then he was in a wood. A thrush was riffling about in last year's leaves. He caught it easily, had its feathers off, and ate it in a couple of crunches. The mate came to investigate. The two birds and their hot blood stayed a craving that was always with him and then he went on, fast, though not running because he knew that brought people after him. In a service station he bought a bottle of water and came out of the shop to see a motorbike roaring to a stop. Ben went to it, pulled by his love for the shining, bright, powerful machine. He stood grinning – his little smile of pleasure. The youth on the machine suppressed any doubts he might have had about this odd-looking bearded man, because he recognized a compatriot in his country, a lover like himself, and he said, 'Watch it a minute,' and went into the shop. When he came out Ben was stroking the handlebars, with a look on his face that compelled this young man who normally would let no one so much as touch his machine, to say, 'Get on, then.' And Ben leaped up and off they went.

'Where are you going?'

'This way,' Ben shouted into the wind.

The great machine growled and roared and bounded along, they were whisking through the traffic, and Ben was roaring too:

it sounded like a song, a shout of triumph, and the youth driving, hearing all this exultation just behind him, laughed and yelled too, and then began singing a real song, which Ben did not know, though he joined in.

Now there was a little town. There the motorbike turned sharply left, and in a moment had left streets behind for country, but Ben was shouting, 'Put me down, I'm going wrong.'

The youth yelled, 'Why didn't you say?' and turned the machine in a dangerous swoop in front of cars and lorries, and they sped back to the town centre. 'Here?' yelled the youth, and Ben shouted, 'Yes.'

He was on the pavement in the middle of the town, and the bike was speeding away, and the youth was giving him the thumbs-up.

Ben set his face to where he knew he must go and walked on, thinking of the motorbike, and his teeth were showing white in his beard, from happiness. They had covered a good distance. Ben would reach where he would have to be hours before he had thought; and in fact he was walking into the road he knew so well by mid-afternoon. There was the house, the big wonderful house, with the garden all around it and there . . . He was looking at windows that had bars on them, and at once a cold but vigorous anger was taking hold of him. Bars: the bars had been for him. He had stood up there shaking those bars with both of his strong fists, and they had not given way at all; only where the bars were set into the walls were bits of paint flaking from all his shaking, showing how little use his strength was. But the anger he felt now was being driven away by a stronger need, pulling him towards the house. His mother, he wanted to see his mother. Because of the kindness of that old lady, he had remembered that other kindness, and understood that that was what it had been: she, like the old lady, had not hurt him, she had come to rescue him from *that place* . . . And out of the front door came small children, running. He did not know them, and thought, Of course, they've moved. His mother wouldn't be here now. He turned away from the house, his home, and began walking this way and that through the streets, like a dog nosing for a scent, but it was not a scent he was after; he had actually seen the other house, the one the family had moved to . . . but wait, there had been another house, after that, and it was the address of that house his mother had put on the big card. It was that house he was moving towards, but it was not what he needed. He had never been to the house where they lived now. He had no way of finding it: he did not have in his mind a pattern of streets, smells, bushes, gates. What now? A desperation like a howl made his chest hurt, and then he thought, Wait, the park, that's where she'll be. And he went to the little park where he had played so often with his brothers and sisters. Or rather, where he had watched them play, because they complained he was rough. When he played it had been by himself, or with his mother.

There was a bench he knew well. His mother loved that park, and that bench, and she would sometimes sit there all afternoon. But the bench was empty. Ben understood one thing, that if he walked about a place for too long people would start noticing him. He did walk about for as long as he dared, glancing into people's faces for 'the look', and then sat on a bench from where he could see *the* bench, which he thought of as his mother's. He waited. He was hungry again. He left the park to find the little café he had used with his gang of mates, the gang he had bossed and led, but the café had gone. He bought a meat sandwich from a machine, and returned to the park, and there he saw her, he saw his mother, sitting with a book in her hand. Her shadow lay across grass almost to where he stood. He was repeating in his mind all the things he must ask her, her new address, his exact age, his birth date, did she have his birth certificate? A loving happiness was filling him like sunlight, and then, ready with his questions, ready to greet her, he saw coming towards her across the park grass – Paul; it was Paul, the brother he had hated so terribly that thoughts of killing him once and for ever had filled hours of his childhood. There he was, a tall, rather weedy young man, with long arms and bony hands, and his eyes – but Ben knew those eyes without having to see them: large, hazy blue eyes. Paul was smiling at his mother. She patted the bench beside her and Paul sat down, and the mother took Paul's hand and held it. A rage so terrible that Ben's eyes darkened and seemed to bleed was shaking him. He wanted to push him down and . . . There was one thing he knew, and he knew it very well, because of so many bad things . . . There were certain feelings he had that were not allowed. Until this rage, this hate, left him alone he could not go anywhere near his mother, near his brother, Paul. But the feelings were getting worse, he could hardly breathe, and through a red glare he watched his mother and that tormentor, that impostor who had always stood between him and his mother, get up and walk away together. Ben followed, but at a good distance. His rage now was being used up by a determination not to be seen. He did not crouch: that was for forests or woods, and he stood upright and walked quietly, well behind the two he followed. Then, there was a house, a rather bigger one than the one they had moved into first, in a garden, and he saw them open a gate, let it swing back, and go together into the house.

Ben was working things out. The house his mother had moved into away from the big house was small. He remembered her saying, 'Big enough for me and Paul.' Which he had understood as *But not big enough for you too.* If she had moved again, and to a bigger house, then that meant the others were there? Or some of them? He knew that they were all grown-up, but what he remembered was the family growing – children growing. In his mind was that other house, crammed with children, and with people. There wouldn't be room for a lot of people in this house . . . He had to simmer down, become calm, lose the need to kill: he walked off around the block, came back, walked about some more, returned, and the front of this new house seemed as blank as an unfriendly face. Then he saw his father walk fast along the pavement. He could have seen Ben by raising his eyes, but he was frowning, preoccupied, and did not look up. Ben knew he could not loiter there for much longer. People noticed, they were always on the watch, even when you thought you saw only blank walls and windows, there were eyes when you did not expect them. He walked around the block again and this time saw Luke going into the house. With him was a small child: the idea that Luke was a father was too much to take in. He was thinking that the family were here, together – his family. He could go in and say, Here I am. And then? He knew they had split up because of him, they quarrelled about him. Only his mother had stood by him. She had come to *that place* where they kept hoses of freezing water coming at him and had taken him home . . . But the others had wanted him to stay there, wanted him dead.

25

It was getting dark. The street lights were out. Friendly night was here. But at night you did not linger too long on a pavement outside a house. He walked past the house, whose lights softly shone at him, *Come in*, and walked back again. He could hear the sounds that meant television. He could go in and sit down and watch the TV with them. And as he thought this he clearly saw how Paul would scream that he could not stay in the same room with him, he saw his father's cold face that always seemed to be turned away from him, Ben. Suppose he just went in and said to his mother, 'Please give me my birth certificate. Just give it to me and I'll go away.' But the rage was pumping up inside him, because all he could see was Paul, who hated him so much. The anger was making his fingers twist and curl; the need to be around that thin neck that would break and crack . . .

He walked away from his family, left it for ever, and the pain he felt cooled his anger. He felt wet damping his beard, and then running through it on his chin. He was so hungry again. He must be careful: night people were different from in the day. Better not risk sitting down at a table . . . He went to a McDonald's, bought a fat juicy lump of meat, threw away the salad and the bun, and ate quickly as he walked. Then he was out of the town, and his face was set for London, for the old woman. He had four pounds left and it was not likely he would have luck again with a motorbike. He was so sad, so lonely, but the dark was his home, night was his place, and people did not look at you so dangerously at night – not, that is, if you weren't in the same room with them. Now he was on a country road, and the sky over him was blurred and soft with stars that had thin cloud running across them. Near him was a little clump of trees, not a wood, but enough to shelter him. He found a bush, settled himself in it, and slept. Once he woke to hear a hedgehog puffing and snuffling near his feet. He could catch it as he sat. What stopped him was not the fear of the prickles in his palms, but a knowledge of prickles on his tongue: you could not bite into a hedgehog as you would a bird. He woke with the first cool breath of dawn. No birds: this was only a thin straggle of trees, and he could see that the houses began quite soon, he could hear traffic. He would reach his part of London about midday. Ahead were hours of his careful, wary walking – and his stomach, oh his stomach, how it begged for food. His hunger hurt and threatened him. It was not an easy hunger: the thin taste of bread or a bun could not satisfy it. It was a need for meat, and he smelled the rawness of blood, the reek of it: yet this hunger was dangerous to him. Sometimes, when he had gone into a butcher's shop, pulled there by the smell, his body had seemed to engorge with wanting, and his arms stretched out of their own accord towards the meat. Once he had grabbed up a handful of chops, and stood gnawing them, the butcher's back being turned, and then the sounds of crunching had made the man whip around – but Ben had run, run – and after that he did not go into these shops. Now he was thinking as he walked of how he could get his hands on meat without spending the four pounds.

His feet were taking him to – he stood outside the tall wire of a building site, looking down into the scene of piled wet earth, machines, men in hard hats. He had worked there for some days, taken on because of those shoulders and arms that could support girders and beams needing two or three men to lift them. The others had stood watching as he shoved and shouldered and lifted.

He had wanted to join with them, their jokes, their talk, but did not know how to. He had never understood, for example, why the way he spoke was funnier than the way they did. Their eyes when they looked at him had been grave, wary. At the end of a week, pay day. These were all men working illegally for one reason or another, and they were paid less than half the union rate. But Ben had earned enough money to take to the old woman, and she had been pleased with him. Two more weeks . . . and a new man had arrived on the job and from the first he had needled Ben, taunted him, grunted and growled. Ben had not at first known that these were meant to be his sounds, nor had he at once understood when the man had pushed and jostled him, once dangerously, when Ben was standing high, streets far below, his feet straddled from beam to beam over space. The foreman had sharply intervened, but after that Ben had kept an eye on this youth, a grinning, careless, show-off redhead, and had tried to keep out of his way. Another week. The money had been paid out inside a little shelter the men used for moments of rest, or when it was raining too badly. He and the redhead had been last in the line to be paid, and this was how his enemy had planned it, for when Ben's envelope was put into his hand, the young man had grabbed it from him and run off, grunting and scratching himself and crouching low and bounding up, and then again: Ben had known this was meant to be a monkey. He had visited the zoo, moving from cage to cage looking at beasts whose names he had been called, ape, baboon, pig-man, pongo, yeti. There was no yeti in the zoo, nor a pongo either, and he had wondered about them, for he knew he was looking for something like himself.

He had looked helplessly at the foreman, hoping he would protect him, and had seen him grinning, and had seen on the faces of the men standing about, their envelopes in their hands, that look, that grin. He had known he would not get help from them. He had worked a full week for nothing. He had been so full of murder that he had had to walk away from it, and had heard the foreman call after him, 'If you're here on Monday, there'll be something for you.' Meaning, not money, but work for those great shoulders of his that had saved them, the others, so much effort. And he was back on Monday, at first looking down into the site, hands on the wire, as if he had been inside it and not out, as if it were a cage, and down there were the men he had worked with, but the redhead had not been there. That was because he had grabbed Ben's money and was afraid to come back. Ben had worked that week slowly, carefully, watching faces, watching eyes, moving out of their way, or positioning himself to take the big weights that were easy for him and not for them. And then, at the end of the week in his envelope had been half the money that was due him. He knew that was half what proper builders got, real workmen, who were not working illegally; but that half was now half again. The foreman had stared him out. It was not the usual foreman, who was sick: this man had come the day before yesterday off another job, to fill in. The men had stood around, watching, their faces kept expressionless. They had been expecting him to complain, make a fuss, even start a fight; they had had their eyes on his big arms and fists. But Ben knew better: he would get the worst of it. He had looked carefully around, from face to face, and had seen them waiting, and had seen, too, that one at least was sorry for him. This man had said something in a low voice to the new foreman, who had simply turned his back and walked away – with the money due to Ben in his own pocket.

On this site, at this place, Ben was owed forty pounds. Yes, the real foreman was there. He was standing a little apart from the others, who were uncoiling cable off a big spool. Ben went down. He saw that first one, and then another, of the men saw him and stopped. The one who had spoken up for him said something to the foreman. What Ben wanted was for that money simply to be given to him and then he could run – he was afraid of these men. Any single one of them he could knock down with a jerk of his elbow, a slap of his hand, but they could all set on him, and that was what made him shiver a little as he stood there. His hair was standing up all over his body. The foreman stood, thinking, then turned half away, pulled out a wad of money, counted some out, gave Ben twenty. And now they all looked to see what he would do, but he did nothing, only walked away. Yet it was here that he had earned money, and had hoped he would again. If he did work here he could expect one or all of them to take his money, and the foreman to cheat him. He turned at the foot of the path up out of the site and saw them uncoiling the cable, still watching him. Up he went, out of their way. He went to Mimosa House. The lift was silent, because it was out of order. Ben went bounding up the stairs, full of happiness because of seeing the old woman. But when he knocked on the door, there was no reply.

A woman opened her door across the landing, and said, 'She's gone to the doctor.' She had the key to the flat, Ben knew that. She and the old woman were friends, and she had often seen Ben going in or out. Now she opened the door for Ben, saying, 'She'll be back soon. There's no saying how long she'll have to wait. She's poorly. I told her she had to get to the doctor.'

Inside, the usually tidy room was disordered. For one thing, the bed had just been pulled up hastily. On it the cat started from sleep, its fur high. Ben did not rummage in the fridge: he hated the cold taste of food just taken out of it, and, too, he did not want to use the old woman's food. He squatted on the bed, ignoring the cat, and looked out. He was waiting for a pigeon to come to the balcony. They often did. The cat turned its head to watch too. A yard apart, not looking at each other, they were united in waiting for whatever might come. The door to the balcony was not locked. Ben set it ajar. It bisected the tiny balcony. Then neither Ben nor the cat moved. At last a pigeon came, but to the wrong part, safe behind the door, and then, soon after, another, to the part where . . . Ben had leaped out, and the bird was in his hand. He was tearing off feathers when he heard the cat's sound, which it always made when a bird was out there, or on the railing, a rusty, hungry noise. Ben ripped some flesh off the bird and flung it down. The cat crept out and ate. The blood was dripping from their mouths. Then there were only feathers blowing about, and some blood stains. The cat went back in. So did Ben. It was not enough, those few mouthfuls of flesh, but it was something, his stomach was appeased. He saw the cat's eyes closing: it was trusting him enough to sleep. Ben curled up on the bed beside the cat, and when Mrs Biggs came in, towards evening, the two creatures were sleeping side by side on her bed.

She took it all in, some feathers clinging to the blood clots on the balcony, the stale smell of blood, that there were only a few inches between Ben's back and the cat's. She wasn't well. She felt bad. Her heart hurt. And she was tired: at the end of a long wait at the doctor's, among grumbling people, she had been given some pills. But what had she been expecting? – she scolded herself – a cure? She set packages down on the table, untied a scarf from her head, drank water from the tap, and then stood for a while looking down at her old big bed – at the cat, at Ben. She lay down along its edge, and watched the shadows come on the ceiling, and then it was dark. Ben slept his noisy, unhappy sleep. The cat was as neat and quiet as – a cat. The old woman dozed off, feeling her heart beat painfully in her side. She woke because Ben was awake, and pressing his back against her.

'Ben,' she said, into the dark. 'I'm not well. I'm going to bed for a day or two to rest up.' He made a sound that meant, I am listening. 'Did you get the certificate?' A silence from Ben, and something like a whimper. 'Did you see your mother?'

'I saw her. In the park.'

She already knew the answer but asked, 'Did you speak to her?' Ben moved against her side, and whimpered again. 'I don't know what to suggest next, Ben. I'd go with you to the place – you know, I told you about, where you get certificates, but I'm not well.'

'I've got some money. I've got twenty pounds.'

'That's not going to get you far, Ben.' He had known she would say that, and he agreed with her.

'I'll get some money.'

She did not ask how. She had been told the story of the building site, how he had been cheated. He would always be cheated, poor Ben, she knew that. And so did he.

When morning came she did not get off the bed, but lay there, breathing slowly and carefully. She said, 'Ben, I want you to go to the bathroom, take off your clothes and wash yourself. You don't smell good.'

Ben did as she said. He had not washed himself in this thorough way before, but he remembered what she did, and did the same. But now he had to put on the dirty clothes.

She said, 'Find your old clothes. They're in that cupboard. Take your new clothes to the launderette, and when you come back here you can put them on again.'

He knew about the launderette. 'How do I get back in again, if you are in bed?'

'The key's on the table. And get some bread and something for you. And be careful, Ben.'

He knew that meant, Don't steal, don't let yourself be carried off into a rage, be on guard.

He did everything as she would have wanted. Then he went to a little shop and bought bread for her – the pale yeasty smell always made him feel a little nauseous – and some meat for himself, and, too, a tin of cat food. All this he did successfully, and let himself back in, and put on his clean clothes. It was mid-morning.

Mrs Biggs was sitting at the table, her hand at her side.

'Make me a cup of tea, Ben.'

He did so.

'And give the cat something.'

He opened the tin he had bought for the cat, and watched it crouch down to eat.

'You're a good boy, Ben,' she said, and tears came into his eyes and she heard him give a sort of bark, which meant he wanted to say thank you to her, expressing his love and gratitude for those words, but he had never heard them, except from her. She almost put out her hand to stroke him as if he were a dog, but he was not a dog, not of that tribe.

She drank her tea, asked for some toast, and lay down again. She slept, the cat by her. There was Ben, in his clean clothes, full of energy and something like happiness because of that loving 'You're a good boy.' He did not want to sleep, but lay on his futon and dozed, hoping she would wake, but she slept all night, and woke in the morning early. Again she asked for this and that, tea, an apple, food for the cat in its saucer. The neighbour came in, saw Ben there, carrying cups and plates into the kitchen, and was pleased for she had defended Ben to the other people on the landing, or who had seen him on the stairs. Now she could say that Ben was looking after Mrs Biggs.

There was a little conference by the bed. The old woman not wanting to get up was a new thing, which the neighbour understood very well, but who was going to look after her? Mrs Biggs asked her to get her pension, for she felt too poorly and – she was apologetic – empty the cat's dirt box. Both women understood that Ben could not do this: the mere idea of it – impossible. Even though the cat's fur was quiet, and she no longer sat with her eyes fixed on Ben. When the neighbour returned with Mrs Biggs' pension she laid the money on the table, and said, looking at Ben: 'That's not enough for more than her and the cat.'

'He's been using his money to buy me things,' said the old woman, but they all knew what the situation was.

'That's all right then,' said the neighbour, and went off to spread the news that the yeti was looking after Mrs Biggs as if he were her son.

And so that time went, a happy time, the best in Ben's whole life, looking after the old woman, even taking her clothes and her bedclothes to the launderette, cooking up dishes from frozen to feed her – but he usually finished them, for she ate so little. But it could not last, because all this time the money was going, going, and he soon had none left. If he wanted to stay there, with Mrs Biggs and the cat, then he would have to get more money and he did not know how. The neighbour, bringing in the pension money, carefully did not look at Ben, and he knew it was a criticism. The old woman did not criticise him, but lay and dozed, or sat and dozed, her hand so often pressing on her heart, saying, 'Ben, we could both do with a cup of tea, I am sure.'

He was hungry, for he was trying to eat as little as he could. It could not go on. He told her he was going to see about a job, and saw her sad little smile. 'Be careful, Ben,' she said. And Ben left: he had no home in this world.

He walked along a street – rather, his feet were taking him up this street, past theatres and eating places – and he was on the side he usually avoided, crossing over before he came to a certain forbidden pavement. This time he did not cross over. He stood outside the theatre which frightened him when it was noisy and full of people, and stood on an empty pavement looking across at a little street where there was a doorway. This was a forbidden place. It was morning, and the cars that worked from the cubbyhole in the wall that called itself Super Universal Cabs were not there yet. They came in from early afternoon onwards. The man who organised these cabs, standing outside his cubbyhole, saying, 'Take them to Camberwell . . . Swiss Cottage . . . Notting Hill . . .' was not there. This man was what Ben feared. It was he who had said, 'Fuck off and don't come back.' His name was Johnston and he was Rita's friend.

Some weeks ago, before Mrs Biggs had found him in the super-market, he had been walking up this pavement, as usual alert for trouble, when he saw a woman in that doorway – that one, next to Super Universal Cabs. She had smiled at him. He followed the smile, went up narrow stairs behind her, and found himself in a room that he knew was poor and ugly, because he was contrasting it with what he remembered of his home, when he still had one, with his mother. The woman, though she was really a girl, for her make-up and big bruised-looking eyes made her look older, stood facing him, her hand on her belt, ready to take it off. She said, 'How long?'

Ben had no idea what she meant, but stood with his teeth bared – this was his scared grin, not the friendly one – and did not reply.

'Ten pounds for a blow job, forty for the whole hog.'

'I don't have any money,' said Ben.

She came over, and put her hands down into his pockets, one on either side, more out of exasperation because of the preposter-ousness of this customer, than expectation, and at this Ben's sexual nature, which he kept down, like all his other impermissible hungers, leaped up, and he gripped her by her shoulders, turned her around and, holding her fast, bent her so that she had to put her hands on the bed for support. He tugged up her skirt with one hand, pulled down her knickers, and took her from behind, short, sharp and violent. He had his teeth in her neck, and as he came he let out a grunting bark, like nothing she had ever heard before. He let her go, and she straightened up, flinging her pale hair off her face and stood looking at his face, then down at his thighs, the hairy thighs. She was not exactly unfamiliar with such hairiness – she had jested with Johnston that some of the men that came to her were like chimpanzees – but it was as if she were trying to find out from those strong furry legs just why this customer was so different. That query, that inspection, not hostile, had something in it that made him again grasp her, bend her over and begin again. He was starved for sex, had been hungry for it a long time, and just as if he had not so recently finished his first bout, his teeth went into her neck and she heard the triumphant grunting bark.

'Just a minute,' she said. 'Just wait a minute.'

She pushed him so that he sat on the bed, and she sat on a chair opposite him. She needed time. This experience – a rape, that was what it amounted to – ought to be making her feel angry, and full of the contempt that she usually felt for her customers, but she had been thrilled by that double rape, the great powerful hands gripping her shoulders, the teeth in her neck, and, above all, the grunt like a roar. She was sitting feeling where his teeth had bitten, but could not find an abrasion. She took out a tiny mirror from her bag, and craned her neck to see – no, the skin was not broken, but it was bruised, and there would be questions from Johnston.

What Ben wanted was to lie on that narrow bed, beside her,

and go to sleep. He was thinking hard. When he was the leader of the gang of boys, the bad boys that everyone was afraid of, there had been girls, and one liked him. She had tried to change him saying, 'But Ben, let's try it this way, turn round, it's not nice what you do, it's like animals.' And he had indeed tried, but could not do what she wanted, for when he was face to face with her the raging angry need to possess and dominate was silent. It came to this – that if they were to do it, then it had to be his way, and soon she resented and even hated him for it. After some attempts she would not see him again, and the word had gone around among the girls that Ben was funny, there was something not quite right with him.

With this girl, Rita, he knew she liked him, and had liked what he did.

A bell rang, or rather hummed from the wall. This was a signal that there was a customer, and that Johnston was downstairs, and in control. She got up, pressed the bell, and said to Ben, 'You've got to go now.'

'Why?' he said. He had not understood at all. He only knew she liked him.

'Because I say so,' she said, as if to a child, thinking that she could not remember talking to a customer like this before. 'Go away.' And then she added, 'If you like, you can come again – in the morning, mind you.' And she pushed him out of the room, and he went down her ugly stairs, zipping himself up, as men so often did on them.

On the pavement a tall rough-looking man took a good sharp look at him, and then looked again – people always looked again.

That was his first visit to Rita and next morning he had gone again. Meanwhile she had told Johnston about him. They were lying on her bed, smoking, very late, after all the minicab custom had ceased. He was her protector, and took a cut, but was not jealous, and was even good to her in a casual careless way. He had examined the bruised places on her neck: teeth marks were visible. He had heard a detailed account of the sex. This was because she wanted to talk about it, he was usually not interested. She had told him it hadn't been like being with a man, more like an animal. 'You know, like dogs.'

'But you like him,' Johnston had said, so that she should mark it and remember that he knew. He was feeling something he believed was not jealousy, more curiosity.

The second occasion was like the first. This time he did it once and she was disappointed, though she could hardly admit this to herself, since she was committed to the creed that her customers left her cold. That roaring triumphant grunt just above her head, the feeling of being helpless in those great hairy hands, the violence of the penetration – well, it thrilled her, but it was too short. She told him so. This was not like being told by that schoolgirl to lie face to face and then, kisses. He understood what she was saying, with his mind at least, and he let his trousers drop, and allowed her to manipulate him. Because this act was so soon after the first, he managed to keep going, and listened to her cries, with curiosity and surprise. But he was pleased, that he pleased her.

Meanwhile, he had no money. Literally, did not have the price of a meatburger, his favourite food. She gave him enough money to eat. It was summer and at night he found a bench or a hallway. She made him wash in her little bathroom. She cut his beard.

This went on for about a month and then Johnston found out she was giving him money and said, 'Now, that's enough, Reet.'

She had become addicted to Ben and his animal ways and did not want to stop. She told a girlfriend, a whore in the next street, about Ben, and took Ben to that room, another poor dingy place, like Rita's. This woman liked what Ben did, though he would have preferred to stay with Rita, and she gave him a couple of quid for his services. But her protector or boyfriend was not complacent, like Johnston, and when he found out told her Ben was not to come near her again. Johnston and he knew each other, and together they warned and threatened Ben.

And so Ben stopped going to Rita, and if he was in that street was careful to stay on the other side, and if he saw Rita, hurried away. It was not being beaten up he feared, for he was sure he could manage Johnston and the other one even if they both came at him together. It was being noticed, drawing attention to himself – that he mustn't do.

A week after that he was seen by Mrs Biggs in the supermarket.

And now, because this was the other place in the world he could go to, and be welcomed with a smile, he made himself cross the tiny street, past Super Universal Cabs, and go up those stairs. The door was closed. He had learned about knocking, because she might have someone else there, but now he let out a shout, like a bull's bellow, and at once the door opened and she pulled him in, slamming the door and locking it.

Rita had been angry with Johnston for sending Ben off. She had reminded him that their agreement was that she would please herself with her customers. The amounts of money she had given Ben were peanuts, nothing compared to what she earned in a day. If that ever happened again – then he should watch out. Johnston knew this was no useless threat. Johnston did not deal only in minicabs, and she knew what he got up to – or thought she did. One word from her to the police – the worst that could happen to her was a fine, and anyway, the police knew about her. She had customers among them. Johnston trusted her, had told her much more than was prudent. Rita, if not the proverbial tart with a heart of gold, was sensible, shrewd, affectionate, and gave him good advice.

Within a minute of arriving in Rita's room, they were at it, and he was like a starved thing. Then, remembering her demands, at once did it again so that she could get her pleasure. And then she said, falling on the bed and pulling him down, 'Where have you been, Ben?'

'He said I shouldn't come here.'

'But I say you can. In the mornings.'

It all started again. He came every morning, and she gave him enough money to eat, and Johnston cross-examined her. 'Why do you like him, Reet? I don't get it.'

She didn't get it either, though she thought enough about Ben. She was not an instructed young woman – or girl, for in fact she was not yet eighteen, Ben's age – but the subject of his age had not come up. She thought he was probably about thirty-five: she liked older men, she knew.

One of the things they had in common, though they did not know it, was that both had had such a hard childhood. She had left school and run away to London from bad parents, had stolen money, been a thief for a while, and then talked the landlord of the building that housed the minicab firm and this tart's room up the stairs into letting her have the room when the previous girl left. She was persuasive. She impressed. She had learned that she usually got her way with people. She had met many different kinds, but nothing like Ben. He was outside anything she had been told about, or seen on the television, or knew from experience. When she saw him naked for the first time, she thought, *Wow! That's not human.* It was not so much the hairiness of him, but the way he stood, his big shoulders bent – that barrel chest – the dangling fists, the feet planted apart . . . She had never seen anything like him. And then there were the barking or grunting roars as he came, the whimpers in his sleep – yet if he wasn't human, what was he? A human animal, she concluded, and then joked with herself, Well, aren't we all?

Johnston did not interfere again, but he was waiting for some opportunity he could turn to his advantage. It came. Ben asked Rita to go with him 'to the place where you get birth certificates'. Rita, familiar with the world of casual work, asked why didn't he try 'to work casual' and the story of the building site came out. Her first reaction was that if anyone cheated Ben then Johnston could sort him out – but knew this would not happen. She asked where Ben had got it into his head he must have a birth certificate, heard about the old woman who said it would help get him unemployment benefit. 'And then what?' Rita asked, really curious about what unnecessarily lawful plans might be fermenting in that shaggy head.

Talking to Johnston, Rita mentioned that Ben wanted a birth certificate so that with it he could enter the world of proper work and unemployment benefit. Johnston saw his chance. He stopped Ben next time he emerged from Rita's room, and said to

him, 'I want to talk to you,' and as Ben crouched, his fists already
clenched up, 'No, I'm not warning you off Reet, I can help you
get your papers.'

Now Johnston went back up the stairs to Rita's, and for the
first time the three of them were together in that room, Johnston
and Rita sitting side by side on the bed, smoking, while Ben
uneasily waited on the chair, wondering if this were a trap, and
Rita had turned against him. He was trying to understand.

'If you have a passport then you don't need a birth certificate,'
said Johnston.

Ben did know that passports were what people took with them
abroad. There had been a trip to France, his father with the other
children, while he stayed with his mother. He could not go with
them, because he couldn't behave as they did.

He said he didn't want to go anywhere, only a paper he could
take to the office where – he described it, as a place where people
were behind glass walls, and in front of them lines of other
people waited for money. It took a long time for him to understand Johnston. In return for a passport, which Johnston could
get from 'a friend who does passports', he, Ben, would make a
trip to France, taking something with him Johnston wanted to
give another friend, probably in Nice, or Marseilles.

'And then shall I come back?'

Johnston had no intention of encouraging Ben to come back.
He said, 'You could stay there a bit and enjoy yourself.'

Ben saw from Rita's face that she did not like this, though she
did not say anything. The idea that he would possess something
that he could keep in his pocket, and show a policeman, or a
foreman on a building site, persuaded Ben, and he went with

Johnston to the machine in the Underground where appeared five little photographs, that Johnston took off with him. The passport, when he was given it, surprised Ben. He was thirty-five years old, it said. He was a film actor: Ben Lovatt. His home address was somewhere in Scotland. Johnston was going to keep this passport 'for safety' but Ben demanded it to show the old woman. Yes, he said, he would bring it back at once.

When he stood outside Mrs Biggs' door he knew the place was empty: he could sense that there was nothing alive in there. He did not knock, but knocked on the neighbour's door, and heard the cat miaow. He had to knock again, and then at last she came to the door, saw him, and said, 'Mrs Biggs is in hospital. I've got her cat with me.' Ben had already turned to go off down the stairs, when she said, 'She'd like it if you visited her, Ben.'

He was appalled: a hospital was everything he feared most, a big building, full of noise and people, and of danger for him. He remembered going to doctors with his mother. Every one of them had had *that* look. The neighbour understood that he was afraid. She and Mrs Biggs had discussed Ben, knew how hard it was for him to inhabit ordinary life – knew for instance that Ben would go down flight after flight of stairs because the lift so intimidated him.

She said, kindly, 'Don't worry, Ben, I'll tell her you came to see her.' Then she said, 'Wait . . .' Left him standing there, returned with a ten-pound note, which she slipped into his breast pocket. 'Look after yourself, Ben,' she said, as the old woman would have done.

Ben made his way back to Rita's. He was thinking about kindness, how it was some people saw him – that was how he put it

– really did see him, but were not put off, it was as if they took him into themselves – that was how it felt. And Rita? Yes, she was kind, she felt for him. But not Johnston: no. He was an enemy. And yet there in Ben's pocket was a passport, with his name in it, and an identity. He was Ben Lovatt, and he belonged to Great Britain which for him until now had been words, a sound, nothing real. Now he felt as if arms had been put around him.

Meanwhile, Rita and Johnston had been quarrelling. She said she didn't like it, what Johnston was doing to Ben. What would happen to him in France? He couldn't speak the language. He could only just cope with things here. Johnston had ended the argument with, 'Don't you see, Reet, he'll end up behind bars anyway.' He meant prison, but Rita heard something else, which in fact Johnston had mentioned during a discussion about Ben: one day the scientists would get their hands on Ben. Rita shrieked at Johnston that he was cruel. She insisted that Ben was nice, he was just a bit different from other people, that's all.

When Ben arrived back in Rita's room, he interrupted this quarrel. In both their minds was the word 'bars', both imagined cages. Johnston did not care what happened to this freak, but Rita was crying. If 'they' got Ben in a cage, he would roar and shout and bellow, and they would have to hit him or drug him, oh yes, she knew how life was, how people were, what one could expect.

Ben sat with his passport in his hand, reluctant to give it back to Johnston, and looked under his deep brows at them and knew it was him they had been quarrelling about. In his family they argued about him all the time. But more than by this angry atmosphere, he was being bothered by the many odours in the

45

room. It smelled of her, the female, but he did not mind that, it was what emanated from Johnston that was making him want to fight or run away. It was a strong, dangerous male smell, and Ben always knew when Johnston had been on the pavement down-stairs, or listening on the stairs, to keep a check on Rita. There were a variety of chemical traces in the air, as sharply differentiated from human ones as traffic stinks from the meat smells coming on to a pavement outside a takeaway. He wanted to get up and go, but knew he must not, until this business was settled. Rita was trying to stop Johnston from doing something.

Rita said to Johnston that he should try and get Ben a job, and 'look after him'.

'Meaning?' said Johnston.

'You know what I mean.'

'I can't stop some bloke tripping him up on a dark night or pushing him under a bus. He upsets people, Reet. You know that.'

'Perhaps he could be one of your drivers?'

'Oh, come on, you're dreaming.'

But now Rita took the passport from Ben, and said she would look after it, and put it into a drawer. Down they went to the cars, which were inserted here and there among the ordinary parked cars.

'Get in,' said Johnston to Ben, opening the door. Ben looked at Rita – Is this all right? – and she nodded. Ben got in behind the driving wheel and at once his face was all delight, exultation. He was thinking of the great glittering roaring accelerating motor-bikes that had been the one joy of his life, like nothing else he had known. And now he was behind a wheel, and could put his hands on it, moving it this way and that. He was making a noise like Brrrr, Brrrr, and laughing.

Johnston pulled Rita into the scene with a hitch of his shoulder, so she was standing right by the driver's seat. He wanted Rita to see, and she did.

'Now turn the key, Ben,' he said.

He did not point the key out to Ben, but Ben's face turned to Rita, for instructions. Rita bent in, touched the key.

Ben fiddled with it, turned it, turned it off as the machine coughed, turned it on, so the car was alive, but grumbled and coughed and died. It was a rackety, cheap third- or fourth-hand car, belonging to a driver who was in between prison sentences for stealing cars.

'Try again,' said Rita. Her voice was actually shaking, because she was thinking, Oh, poor Ben, he's like a three-year-old, and somewhere she had been foolishly believing that he could learn this job. Ben's hairy fist enclosed the key, and shook it, the car came alive, and now Ben began a pantomime of shifting gears, for he knew that that was what you had to do. It was an automatic.

'Now,' said Johnston, leaning right in, and pointing to the lever. 'I'm going to show you what to do with that.' And he did, again and again. 'You squeeze these little side pieces together – see? Then let the brake go – now do it. Then, be careful, watch to see if a car is coming.' All this was silly; Ben could not see, could not do it. He was making his fist close up tight, watching Johnston's hand, pulling his hand back and then putting it forward near the brake, but he wasn't really doing it, because he couldn't. As Johnston had known.

Rita was crying. Johnston straightened up from the window,

and opened the door, and said to Ben, 'Get out.' Obedient, Ben got out, not wanting to; he wanted to go on sitting there playing at being a driver. Then Rita said to Johnston, 'You're cruel. I don't like that.'

She went into her doorway, not looking at him or at Ben. Johnston pretended to find work in his cubbyhole, though no customers had turned up, and Ben followed Rita up the stairs.

It was better up there now Johnston's powerful odours had gone, leaving only memories in the air.

Rita said to Ben, 'You don't have to go anywhere, if you don't want to.' She sounded sulky, offended, but that was because she was angry at having cried. She did not like showing weakness, and particularly not in front of Johnston.

'Sit down, Ben,' she said, and he sat on the chair while she painted her face to hide the marks of tears. Then she made up her eyes again, to look enormous, with the black and green paints. This was so customers would not notice her face, which was not pretty, but pale, or even white, because she was never really well.

'Why does it say I am a film actor?' asked Ben.

Rita simply shook her head, defeated, by the difficulty of explaining. She knew he did not go to the cinema, and was able to put herself in his place enough to know that reality was more than enough for him, he could not afford to complicate that by pretence. She did not know that it was the building itself which frightened him: the dark inside, the rows of seats where anybody might be, the tall lit screen, which hurt his eyes.

In fact she had been impressed by Johnston arranging with 'his friend' to have *actor* on the passport. Actors did not work all the time. They were often idle. She had actors among her customers:

to be out of work was no crisis for them, though it might be a worry. Ben looked out of the ordinary, but you expected pop stars and actors to look amazing. No, it was a brilliant strategy. In a crowd of film people or the music scene, Ben would not be so conspicuous. But what was Johnston up to? She knew it could be nothing good.

And yet something had to be done about Ben. It was late summer now, but soon it would be autumn, and then winter. Ben had twice been moved on from his favourite bench by the police. What was he going to do in winter? The police knew him. All the homeless and down-and-out people must know him. Probably Johnston was right: Rita had not been to France, but she had been to Spain and Greece, and could imagine Ben more easily in a tapas bar, or a taverna, than a London pub. But Johnston wasn't concerned for Ben's well-being, she knew that.

That night, late, when her last customers had gone, and the minicab drivers had gone home, when it was more morning than night, and Ben was crouching in a doorway in Covent Garden, she asked Johnston what he intended for Ben, and when she heard she was angry and tried to hit Johnston, who held her wrists and said, 'Shut up. It's going to work, you'll see.'

Johnston planned to make Ben carry cocaine – 'A lot, Reet, millions' – across to Nice, not concealed at all, but in ordinary holdalls, under a layer of clothes. 'Don't you see, Reet? Ben is so amazing the narks will be trying to figure him out, they won't have time for anything else.'

'And when he gets there?'

'Why should you care? What's he to you? He's a bit of rough for you, that's all.'

'I'm sorry for him. I don't want him to get hurt.'

This was where, in the previous exchange, the word 'bars' had arrived. 'Bars' were imminent again.

'He couldn't manage an aeroplane, he couldn't manage luggage, what's he going to do in a place where people don't speak English?'

'I've thought of everything, Reet.' And he detailed his plan.

Rita had to admit that Johnston had thought of everything. She was impressed. But suppose the plan did succeed, at the end of it Ben would be alone in a foreign country.

'I don't want him hanging around here. People notice him. The police want an excuse to close me down. They don't like the cabs being here. I keep telling them, you may not like us, but the public do. I could keep twice the number of cabs busy, if we had parking space. But they are just putting up with me and waiting for an excuse. And Ben is like a big notice saying, "Here is trouble". And I'm scared of him starting another fight. One of the drivers said something and Ben knocked him down.'

'What did he say?'

'He called him a hairy ape. I stopped the fight. But – I want you to understand, Reet.'

Rita had to concede the justice of all that. But there was more: Johnston was jealous. 'Funny thing,' she said. 'You've never been jealous of anybody. But you are of him.'

He didn't like this, but at last grinned a little, not pleasantly, and said, 'Well, I can't compete, can I? Not with a great hairy ape?'

'He's a lot more than that.'

'Listen, Reet, I don't care. I've had enough of him.'

Johnston's plan began with taking Ben to shops, good ones,

and buying good clothes. No more stuff from charity shops. Buying jeans, trousers, underclothes – that was easy: but those shoulders, that chest, the heavy arms – in the end Johnston decided on a bespoke tailor, and got him shirts that fitted, and a couple of jackets.

'And what is all that going to cost?' asked Rita.

'I told you, there's millions in this.'

'Dream on.'

'You'll see.'

Next, Ben was taken to a barber. He wished the old woman could see him now: she had said he would look good, and he knew he did. The barber had exclaimed over the double crown, but by the time he had finished who could notice?

Now Johnston took Ben up for a flight over London in a small plane, to get him used to flying. At first Ben's eyes rolled in his head and he gave a roar of fear, as he looked down, but Johnston was sitting beside him, behaving as if nothing was wrong, and he said, 'Look Ben, do you see that? It's the river, you know the river. And look, there's Covent Garden. And there's Charing Cross Road.' Ben took it all in and told Rita about it. 'When can I do it again?' he wanted to know.

'You are going to do it again. In a big plane. Soon.'

And then, she thought, I'll probably not see you again . . . She was fond of him, yes, she was. She was going to miss . . . She permitted, no, invited, quite a few of the extraordinary fucks that were like nothing she had experienced. She knew very well that it was not in his nature that these could lead to tenderness. There was no connection between those short violent acts of possession and what happened even seconds later, when it was as if nothing at all had happened. And yet, once when she had allowed him to stay the night, he had nuzzled up to her in his sleep, that hairy face pushing into her neck, and he had licked her face and her neck. She supposed he was fond of her. He asked if she was coming to France too, but what did he imagine when he said *France*?

'It's the same as here, Ben,' she tried to explain. 'There's a nice blue sea, though. You know what sea is?'

Yes, he did; he remembered going with his family to the seaside.

'Well, then, it's like that. Like here only the sea is right close.' She found some postcards of Nice, of that coast, and he puzzled over them: she knew he did not see what she saw. And she had not said that there would be a different language, different sounds.

Rita was leaning in her doorway, dressed for the part in black leather and black fishnet stockings, watching Johnston wave people to the minicabs, directing the drivers – the usual scene on this pavement from mid-afternoon till twelve or one in the morning, as people came from theatres and restaurants, when she saw a man she did not like the look of come up to Johnston, confront him. Johnston was afraid, she knew. In her experience trouble always started like this: a man appeared from nowhere with a certain look about him that said, 'Look out!' – and then something bad happened. When this man had taken himself off, she saw Johnston sweating, leaning on his cubbyhole counter, taking quick gulps from a bottle kept there. Then he saw her, took in her concern, and said, 'We've got to talk, Reet.'

That night she made sure the door on the street that led up to her room was locked, and invited Johnston up. She lay on her bed, propped against pillows, one leg dangling – a pose she had evolved to excite customers – smoking, and watched Johnston shifting and fidgeting on his chair. He was smoking, and took frequent mouthfuls from his whisky flask. The stale smoky air was making her cough.

She knew his story – most of it. He had run away at fourteen from a bad home. He had done a spell in borstal, then lived rough, kept himself by shoplifting and thieving. A year in prison. That over, he went straight for a time, but a sentence for robbery with violence took him back. He had finished that five years ago. Wheeling and dealing, at first just ahead of the law, but then in deep, and deeper, involved in a dozen scams, which became increasingly dangerous, he was aided by the skills he had learned in prison and because he was known in the criminal community. The minicab business did well enough, but it had never been much more than a front. She was not surprised that he was in trouble, and when he said, 'I'm in a trap, Reet,' imagined a debt or two, perhaps blackmail. But now, as he began to tell her, strengthening himself with large gulps of whisky – he was a bit drunk – she sat up on the edge of the bed, and stared at him.

'What are you saying? What are you telling me?'

He had been persuaded by a man on the fringes of respectability to try his luck on the stock exchange – futures. You couldn't lose, this friend said. There was money, if you kept your head. Well, they had kept their heads but not their money.

'You're telling me you owe a million pounds?'

'That's nothing, Reet. A million's nothing to that lot.'

'Well, it's a lot to you.'

'True,' he said, and drank.

'So. You're afraid of going back to prison?'

'Right on. That's what I'll be doing, if I can't get some real money.'

'Let's get this straight. *You* owe a million, or the two of you together?'

'He owes much more. He was in deeper than me. He did me a bit of a favour really, he let me in – but now if I don't give him a million he's going to shop me and I'll go down.'

She lay back again, and coughed. 'Fucking pollution,' she said. 'Sometimes this room's so full of stink from the street I can't breathe.' The cigarette smoke thus being neatly excused, she lit another, and threw Johnston one.

'OK,' she said. 'But if you don't get away with this cocaine deal, if they catch you, you'll go down anyway. For life probably.'

'That's right, but I'm going to get away with it.'

'So before you even start to get some money for yourself you've got to pay back a million?'

'When the stuff arrives in Nice, that's the million paid. And the rest is for me.'

'Nothing for Ben?'

'Oh, I'll see him right.'

'And how about me?' she enquired. 'Aren't I taking any risks?'

'You won't know what's in those cases, Reet. I'm going to make sure of that.'

'When they nab Ben, and ask him where he got the stuff, he'll say from me. Because he knows me better than he knows you, and he trusts me. So he'll say it was me.'

A silence.

'But he knows that he is taking something from me to a friend in France.'

A silence.

'From *me*, Reet.'

'But I'm in it too, aren't I? Ben doesn't know enough to lie well. We can't count on him. He'll say it was me and you.'

Johnston cut this knot with, 'You just tell me something. How do you see yourself, Reet? You don't fancy this life – so I've heard you say, haven't I? Well, you stand by me in this and I'll see that you get out of this life, for good.'

'You'll see me right, like Ben?'

Now Johnston leaned forward, waving away swathes of cigarette smoke, and spoke to her – she saw clearly enough – from the heart. 'Look, you and I have gone along together – how long now, Reet? Three years? I haven't let you down ever – well, have I?'

'No, you haven't.'

'Well then?'

He continued to lean forward, all drunken appeal, desperate, his reddened eyes wet – from the smoke? From tears?

'It's such a gamble,' she said. 'You're taking such a chance.'

'I've got to, Reet. If I get away with this, then I'm clear for the rest of my life.'

She lay back again, this time with her two legs straight in front of her, and stared at him, and thought she didn't know which of them she was more sorry for, Johnston, who she knew had it in him to be better than he was – she knew because this was true of her, too – and who had such a power to impress people, looking as he did like Humphrey Bogart – well, most of the time he did, a little at least, but not now when he was drunk and stupid – or Ben, who was being sent off into such danger, to save Johnston.

But when she came to think of it, and she was thinking hard now, she owed more to Johnston than to Ben. She supposed she could say Johnston was her man: she didn't have another, after all. And it was true, he had been good to her. And what he said was true, that she hated this life and had several times thought of doing herself in. 'Better do myself in before some sex maniac does it for me.' She knew she probably wouldn't last long, anyway. She was unhealthy. Her skin was bad. Her hair when not dyed silver-blonde was a coarse limp black mess: you had only to touch it to know she was sick. When she was not made up, not dressed for the kill, she looked at herself in the glass – and put on her make-up as fast as she could.

Now she thought, Right! Suppose they do catch Ben and send me down, it couldn't be much worse than this life. And she decided to help Johnston. In every way she could.

And now Johnston took Ben through what would happen at the airport. When he was finished, Rita repeated it all, again and again.

Everything was going to depend on Johnston's 'friend' – 'I knew him in prison, Reet, he's all right' – he would be with Ben at the airport and then on the plane and then go with him into Nice and look after him.

'And how much are you paying him?'

'A lot. When you put everything together, and add it all up – clothes for Ben, the luggage, the trip on the aeroplane, the passport – that was a hundred for a start – and Richard – that's the contact – then it all adds up. And there's the hotel, too. But even so it's peanuts compared with what there's in it for us.'

'Well, don't spend it before you have it, that's all.'

'Look, Reet, I know you think I'm barmy, but it'll work, you'll see.'

'Luck, that's all,' said Rita. 'They have sniffer dogs, they check the luggage.'

'Sometimes they do. But they aren't going to bother with a load of tourists going to Nice. And that goes for the French narks too. They'll be watching planes from Colombia and the East, not a nice little harmless plane from London.'

There was one thing Rita didn't know. The plan was for three cases: one very big, stuffed with packets of cocaine, with a layer of clothing over it, which would be checked in at the desk; one with Ben's things in it; and one to take on the plane. When Rita heard that Johnston planned to fill this one too with the deadly packets, possibly heroin, she screamed, she shouted, she even assaulted him, so he had to hold her fists. 'You know they pick cases to check, just at random, they could easily pick Ben's take-on case.' He soothed her and promised her, said he wouldn't do it, if she was upset about it, but in fact he did not keep this promise: Ben was to go through to the plane and on to it carrying the dangerous case.

'The whole thing is mad,' Rita kept saying. 'And poor Ben – it's cruel, I think. Just imagine him in prison.'

'It's just because he's so weird that it's going to work.'

It did work. There was a period while Johnston and Rita could not believe how much things were changing; the difference between their circumstances now, and what was possible to them was too great. Johnston was not so stupid to allow large sums of money to appear in a bank account, but large sums found their way deviously to him over the next few months. He gave Rita enough to buy a restaurant in Brighton, which did well. She could have married, but did not. Sometimes Johnston came to see her, meetings precious to them both, since only they understood how narrowly they had escaped lives of prison and crime.

Johnston had seen on a television programme that it was easy to buy a title and right to land from impoverished (and surely cynical?) aristocrats, for sums that now seemed to him negligible. He did this, became a lord of a manor, but was soon restless and knew he had made a mistake. He did not like doing nothing. He became owner of a very superior car-hire firm, chauffeuring the rich and the famous, mostly around London, and employed the kind of person whom once he would have thought of as far above him. He enjoyed his life, loved his Rolls-Royces and Mercedes, and cultivated respectability. His children, when he got them, went to good private schools. So you could say that this part of our tale had a happy ending.

On the morning of the great gamble Ben was dressed by Rita – Johnston supervising – in a bespoke shirt and a good jacket. Rita was crying, when Johnston put Ben into one of the minicabs, and instructed the driver exactly what to do. The last thing Ben said was, 'When am I coming home?' 'We'll see,' said Johnston, and Rita turned away so Ben would not see her guilty face.

He allowed himself to be driven to Heathrow, though he was feeling sick. The driver parked in Short-term Parking, and got a trolley for the bags, a black one, a red one, a blue one. He took Ben to the club-class check-in desk, handed in Ben's passport, took it back with the boarding pass, and nudged Ben when he was asked if he had forbidden items, and if he had packed the bags himself. Rita had told him over and over again that he must say that yes, he had packed them himself. He remembered, after a hesitation. The check-in girl had taken in 'Film Actor' on the passport, and was staring at Ben during her ministrations to his cases and the boarding card. This stare did not discompose Ben, he was so used to it. The driver, a Nigerian, who was being paid a good bit extra, walked with Ben to Fast Track, gave him his carry-on case, the blue one, his passport and the boarding card, and told him, 'Go through there.' When Ben hesitated he gave Ben a little push, and stood back to watch him go, so he could report back.

Ben was by himself, and he was terrified, his mind whirling with everything he had to remember. He showed his boarding card to the official, who glanced at it, and stared at him, and went on staring until the next traveller claimed his attention. Now there was a difficult bit. Over and over again Rita and Johnston had told him what to do. Ahead would be a kind of black box, with an opening that had things hanging down. He must go to it and put his case on the shelf there. The case would disappear into the opening, and he must look for the metal arch, close to, go through it when told, and then a man would search him, feel his pockets and down his thighs. Ben had said, 'What for?' And they had said, 'Just to make sure you're all right.' The word 'guns' would have scared him. This was the part Rita feared most, because she knew how unpredictably Ben reacted to being touched.

Ben saw the machine ahead. It seemed to him frightful, and he wanted to run away. He knew he must go on. There was no one waiting to help him. He stood with his case in his hand, helpless, until a man behind him said, 'Put it there – look.' And when Ben did not move he took the case and put it into the machine. This unknown helper went ahead of him to the arch, since Ben hesitated, and so Ben saw what he had to do.

Meanwhile his holdall was moving through the x-ray machine. Under the top layer of clothing, among paper packets of the terrible white powder, were inserted here and there toilet things, scissors, a nail-file, clippers, a razor – all in metal which would show up on the screen. But this was the key moment, when ill-luck might lay its hands on Ben and – unless Ben remembered, when interrogated, never to say Rita's name or Johnston's – on them too.

If the girl at the x-ray machine was doing her job, absorbed in it, the official whose job it was to frisk Ben hardly touched him. He was staring at the shoulders, the great chest, thinking, Good God! What *is* this? Ben was grinning. It was from terror, but what this official saw was the smile of a celebrity used to being recognised – he saw plenty of celebrities. If he had laid his hands closely on Ben he would have found him trembling, sweating, cold – but he waved Ben on. Now Ben had to remember to retrieve his case from the machine's exit. He did not know that here was his moment of greatest danger: descriptions of what he had to do were not put to him in terms of danger. But luck held: 'Is this your case, sir?' was not said to Ben, but to the man coming after him. Ben stood there grinning, and then, understanding at last that this blue case jiggling there beside him was his, remembered instructions, took it up and went on towards . . . He was in a daze, and a dazzle, feeling sick and cold. This great space with its lights, its crowds, the shops, the colours, so much movement and noise – in any case it would have frightened him, but he knew that he must remember, must remember . . . He was on the edge

of sending out little whimpers of helplessness, but then he saw
that just ahead a man behind a desk was waving him on and he
must show his passport. It was in his hand. How had it got there?
He couldn't remember . . . But the official merely glanced at it
and back at Ben. What he was thinking was, If he is a film star
then I've never seen him in anything.

Now Ben was standing well beyond the line of passport desks
and he did not know what to do next. He had been told there
would be someone there looking out for him, Johnston's friend,
and yes, there he was, a young man was hurrying forward, scared
eyes on Ben's face.

It was at this point that something happened that had not been
foreseen. Johnston – had he been watching – would have said,
'That's it! I've done it!' Barring some really unfair bad luck he
would shortly be the owner of several million pounds sterling.

The young man, Ben's minder, was – literally – shaking with
relief, and from the reaction. He arrived directly in front of Ben,
trying to smile, saying hurriedly, 'I'm Johnston's friend, I'm
Richard.'

Ben said, 'I'm cold. I want my jersey.' He put down the holdall,
and tried to unzip it, not seeing at first the tiny lock. He said,
'Where is the key? Why is it locked up?'

Richard Gaston (but he had many names in his life) had arrived
in London yesterday on the ferry from Calais, and had spent hours
with Johnston being given instructions for this day's events, and
for afterwards, in Nice. He travelled out to Heathrow on the
Underground, stood at a distance watching the scene with the
minicab driver and Ben at check-in, had gone separately through
passport control and customs, with the economy travellers, had

waited for Ben to emerge, all the time enlarging his ideas of himself with reflected glory from Johnston, who was so clever. He had had many doubts about this scene, just like Rita, but look, it had succeeded.

And here was Ben, bending down, tugging at the zip, pulling at the lock. It was evident that those hands could tear the holdall apart, if Ben decided to do it that way. Richard imagined those packets scattered everywhere, the security people coming up . . .

'I'm cold,' said Ben.

It was a warm afternoon and Ben already had a jerkin on over his shirt – a very posh shirt, as Richard noted.

'You can't be cold,' was Richard's injudicious order to Ben. 'Now, come on. We've cut it a bit fine. They're boarding. Don't be difficult, now.'

These words had an effect which caused Richard to jump back and away from Ben, who was apparently about to grip him by the arms and then . . . Ben was seething with rage.

'I want my jersey!' shouted Ben. 'I've got to have my jersey!'

Richard was scared, but not numbed by it. He was rallying himself. He had been told that Ben was a bit funny . . . he had moods . . . he had to be humoured . . . he was a bit simple. 'But he's all there, so don't treat him like a dummy.'

These descriptions of Ben, scattered through the hours of discussion with Johnston, seemed to Richard all off the point. Johnston would call this 'a mood', would he? Richard was sending nervous glances all around. Was anyone watching? Well, they soon would, if Ben went on shouting.

If that zip broke, if that little lock sprang open . . .

Richard said, gasping, 'Listen, Ben, listen, mate. We're going to miss the plane. You'll be OK in the plane. They'll give you a blanket.'

Ben stood up, letting the holdall fall. Richard couldn't know it, but it was the word 'blanket' that reached him. The old woman had used to say, 'Take this blanket, Ben, wrap yourself up a bit. The heating's a bit low tonight.'

Richard saw that things had changed: Ben was no longer breathing pure murder. Now, unwittingly, he added to his advantage, 'Johnston wouldn't want you to spoil it now. You've done good, Ben. You're right on. You're a bit of a wonder, Ben.'

It was the word *good*.

Ben picked up the holdall, went with Richard along the corridors, the moving pavements, to the right places. It had all been nicely judged: they would be in the middle of the crowd of people boarding. At the desk Ben found his passport and boarding card in his hand, put there by this new friend, who had taken them from him, it seemed, while they argued – Ben had let them fall as he wrestled with the zip and the lock – and then on they walked, along and down and around and down, and then there was a door and by it a smiling female, who directed the two to club class. Ben stood helpless in the aisle, and Richard took the case from him and slid it up into the bin, feeling as if he were handling a snake. He had told Johnston that on no account would he touch that case, so that he could tell any interrogator that he knew nothing about it, but now he saw how foolish that had been. Ben was in his seat, the seatbelt was fastened across him, and Richard was about to ask for a blanket, and then explain to Ben about the take-off, the flight – there would be clouds underneath them and then . . . But Ben had fallen asleep.

What a good thing, thought Richard. What a relief.

Ben slept until they landed and people were getting off. Ben was dazed and it seemed he hardly knew who Richard was. He forgot the precious case when the time came to stand up and pull it down. Richard hauled it down for him, and carried it all the way to the luggage carousel. Almost at once the great black bag appeared – the dangerous one – and then the red one, with Ben's things in it.

'When are we going on the plane?' asked Ben. He had expected something like the trip he had made with Johnston over London in the little plane.

Richard did not answer: ahead was the last hazard, Customs, but they were not bothering. In a moment the two were out in the sunshine, and then, with the bags, in a taxi. Richard was sitting back in his seat, eyes closed, still shaking with the terror of it all. He knew very well that it was only luck that had saved them even while he thought admiringly of Johnston. He wanted badly to sleep: he understood why Ben had gone to sleep, from strain, on the plane. During that ride, Ben was silent. For one thing, his eyes hurt, because of the glitter of the sun on the sea – he did not at first understand that great scoop of shining blue, which was nothing like the seaside at home. He felt sick, too: he hated cars, he always had. Then they were on a pavement, with people everywhere, and Richard led Ben to a table where he sat, pushing a chair towards him. Ben sat, as if this might be a trap, and the chair could close around him like jaws. It was mid-afternoon. They were under a little umbrella but the tiny patch of shade did not do much for Ben's painful eyes. He sat with them half-closed. The waiter came: coffee for Richard, but Ben wanted orange juice, he hated coffee. Cakes came, but Ben never did like cake much, so Richard ate them. And there they sat, hardly talking, Ben trying to take in what he could of the glitter and clamour of the scene around him through half-closed eyes. It was a busy street, and a busy café, and no one was taking any notice of them. Then, suddenly, a man appeared by the table, and Richard said to him, 'The black one and the blue one.' Ben watched as this person, an apparition composed of bright light and noise, disappeared towards a taxi with the two cases. Only Ben and Richard watched. No one else, whether idling on the pavement, or sitting at the café tables, or driving past, so much as glanced at the two cases, one very large, one of an ordinary size, whose contents would soon be added to the rivers of poison that circulate everywhere in the world. Ben was confused. He had thought the blue one, that he had carried through the machines and the officials, was his, but it seemed not. This red one was his. And there was something else that he was at last just beginning to take in – he had been too confused to understand. All around him people were talking loudly, but he did not understand what they said. Rita had told him that everyone would talk French, but it was all right, Johnston's friend was British and would talk English and look after him – but he had not known that he was going to sit at a table in this foreign country understanding nothing, but nothing, of what was going on around him. And that man, the one who had gone off with the bags, had understood Richard talking English, but to the taxi driver he had spoken in French. Exhaustion was numbing Ben again.

'And so that's that,' said Richard, and he had to say it, to mark or define the accomplishment of the deed, but he knew Ben had no idea of what had happened.

'I'm going to take you to the hotel,' he said to Ben.

A lot of discussion had gone into the choice of hotel. Rita had said, a cheap one, where people are friendly – meaning herself. Johnston had said, 'No, a good hotel. They'll speak English. In a cheap hotel they'll only speak French.'

'He won't know how to cope with a good hotel,' said Rita, but she was wrong. It all went brilliantly. Ben had only to sign his name at the hotel desk, while people smiled at him, because he was a film star, and then followed by smiles he was led to a lift by Richard. He hesitated there because of his fear of lifts, but Richard pushed him into it, and it was only two floors, no more than a moment. In his room he was at once at ease, because it reminded him of his childhood, his home. So much was this so that he looked at the window to see if there were bars. Then he went to them, to look out: much lower down than the windows of Mrs Biggs' flat in Mimosa House, Halley Street. He strolled about the room, the grin gone from his face, and Richard, slumped into a chair, watching, knew that everything was going to be easy. All he had to do was show Ben the bathroom and how the shower worked, and the air conditioning. Then he said that he must go, but he would be back soon to take Ben to supper.

He left Ben sitting in a chair looking up through open windows at a blue, hot sky.

He telephoned Johnston, but only said, 'It's OK – yes, it's all right.'

Johnston heard this, and at once ran up Rita's stairs to tell her, and went off into fantasies of doing it all again: he would fetch Ben back, and repeat the triumph. But Rita brought him down to earth. 'Stop it, Johnston. You've got away with it this time.'

When Richard returned, Ben was splashing and shouting in the shower, apparently quite happy, but the first thing he said, as he came out to dry himself and get dressed, was, 'When can I go back home?'

Richard took him to a proper restaurant, mostly because he wanted to eat well for once: he was having a thin time of it. But he might just as well have gone to a McDonald's. Ben would only drink juice, and, saying he was hungry, ate a big steak, leaving the *frites* and the salad, and then wanted another. Afterwards Richard took him strolling along the front, to look at the sea, then another café, then to an evening show with dancing and singing. Richard could not make out what Ben thought of it all: he agreed to everything but only when he was eating seemed to show real enjoyment.

At the hotel Richard counted some money into Ben's hand, and said, 'You won't need it, but in case. And I'll be here early tomorrow.' His orders were to see that Ben could manage ordinary day-to-day things. Then he took a big packet of money down to the hotel safe, and checked it, in Ben's name, for he knew, from watching Ben's unobservant ways, that if he carried that money, thieves would have had it all off him in a day.

Richard's programme for keeping Ben amused was really arranged for himself: that was why he hired a car to take Ben on a trip to the hilltowns behind Nice. But Ben was sick, and when they reached some charming little square or restaurant, did not want to sit outside; he looked for shade, and even then kept his eyes closed most of the time. It was clear that he had to have dark glasses, and so back in Nice he tried some on but none seemed right. Richard took him to a proper oculist who, on examining Ben's eyes, seemed uneasy, even incredulous, and asked a good many questions. He said it was difficult to prescribe for eyes he described as 'unusual', but at last Ben did say he liked a pair. Now, with the glasses, he drew even more stares and, fidgeting and uneasy, kept saying, 'Somewhere else. Not here. I don't like it here.'

Then, as they walked towards their reflections in a shop window, he stopped, bent forward, looking at himself. 'No eyes,' he said, in explanation. 'No eyes. My eyes have gone.' And he panicked, taking off his glasses. 'But Ben, look at me, then I've got no eyes as well.' And Richard whipped off his sunglasses, showing Ben his eyes, and put them back on. Ben slowly replaced his. But stood looking at himself. What he was seeing was very different from anything he could have seen in London: that smart linen jacket, his hair, and now, his blacked-out eyes.

Richard gave up his plans for trips into the countryside behind that dazzling coast and tried to find what Ben would enjoy. What did he like, though? He seemed to be pleased, strolling about, or sitting in cafés where people lazed and chatted. It was that ease with each other, the carelessness of it, that was attracting Ben, but Richard did not know that. He could think only in terms of his own past, and wondered if Ben was scared, thinking he was being followed. Ben did very much like walking along the edge of the sea, seeing the ships that appeared and were there, and then were not there, for they went again. He said to Richard, 'Where do they go?' 'Who?' 'Those ships?' 'Oh, everywhere. All over the world, Ben.'

And he saw Ben's uncomprehending face.

He liked mealtimes, and his steaks and fruit – that was all he ate, steak and fruit. He knew how to sit at a café table and order what he wanted, and he was managing the hotel well, sending out his clothes to be laundered, and going himself to the hotel barber, where he was shaved and his hair trimmed. Richard took him one evening to a nude show, but he got so carried away, letting out yelps and shouts of excitement, that Richard had to shush him. He wanted to go the next night, and promised to sit quietly, but when the girls came on, their nakedness bedecked with wisps of feather or shining stuff, he forgot, and had to be held down in his seat. Richard was actually afraid that Ben would run up to the stage and drag off some girl.

What was Ben? He slept in his bed, like everyone else, he used his knife and fork, he kept his clothes clean, he liked his beard neat, and his hair cut, and yet he was not like anybody.

During that week the inhabitants of this ancient port, all well used to criminals and adventurers, had taken Richard's measure; he was probably the local mafia, this young man – but not as young as he tried to seem – good-looking in an ingratiating way, a manner that always had threat in it, no matter how much he smiled. But they could not place Ben. People made excuses to get into conversation. 'Who is he?' Some said, '*What* is he?' All they could get out of Richard, who was becoming proud of his ability to fend them off, was, 'He's a film star.' And soon, as this seemed to go down well, 'He's famous. He's Ben Lovatt.'

At the end of a week Richard telephoned Johnston to say that Ben could not manage by himself. He needed another week of surveillance. Johnston did not yet know how triumphantly his plans were working. A first instalment of money had come through, but he was going to have to wait for the next one, because of arousing suspicion. He did not want to pay Richard for another week, thought his accomplice had already been promised more than enough, a quarter of a million pounds, which to Johnston would quite soon seem nothing much. Richard had argued that if he was picked up by the police with Ben going through French customs then he would be in the sort of trouble that would put him in prison for years. Now Johnston said that he hadn't been arrested, everything was fine. 'No,' said Richard now, 'but I might have been.' He wanted another quarter of a million. 'Without me it wouldn't have worked.' 'Yeah, but I'm not short of people to do my dirty work,' said Johnston, determined not to give way to Richard, probably beginning a process of blackmail.

This conversation could not go on: it was on a telephone, not in the cubbyhole but in the office of a friend of a friend, and even so, it could be traced.

'What difference is another week going to make?' asked Johnston.

'It depends if you want him nicked or not,' said Richard. 'He just does whatever I tell him, so it'll be the same with anybody, won't it?'

Traffic was swirling and grinding all around Richard: he was shouting. Johnston, in the quiet of a room in a Brixton back street that called itself an office, lost his temper, and shouted instructions, the most important being that if Ben did insist on coming back, he must not know where he could find either him, Johnston, or Rita. Then he agreed to pay for another week.

Richard told Ben that they would have another week's holiday.

'And then are we going home?' asked Ben.

'What do you want to go back there for? Why do you want to leave all this?'

For Richard this coast had been a revelation of well-being. He had come from a northern English town, and an ugly background: you could say he had been born a criminal. Like Johnston he had been in borstal, and then in prison. Meeting Johnston was the luckiest thing that ever happened to him. He worshipped Johnston, was eager to do anything for him. He was sent to this coast by Johnston, for not too delicate negotiations about getting a car, a Mercedes, into France, without papers, had succeeded and stayed. The life, particularly the casual comings and goings of the cafés and restaurants, the sunshine, the skies of this coast, bathed him with promises of happiness. He had been living poorly, hardly able to eat, though it was worth it for the sake of living here. And now this little crook, because of Johnston, was going to have a quarter of a million pounds and planned to buy a small house, or a flat, anything, provided he would be here, on the edge of this sea, where the light was.

And here was Ben, who always had to sit in the shade, and who wanted only to go back to London – but Richard had no idea at all how much.

During that second week, one night when Ben had been left at the hotel, by Richard, he set off by himself and wandered into the streets, going up the steps, always higher into the town, until he was stopped because there, in a doorway, was a girl and she was smiling at him.

71

She established that he was English, and then, using her few words in English to set the price, turned to go into her room. Ben did not have in his pockets what she had asked for; which was much more than Rita demanded. He thought that she would be the same as Rita, and be good to him. In the room, this girl examined Ben: she was enough like Rita to admire those great shoulders, the power of him. She turned away to slip off her skirt, and felt those hands on her shoulders, and that she was being bent forward, and the teeth in her neck. She struggled free, and screamed that he was a *cochon*, an animal, a pig, a *bête*, pushed him towards the door and out of it, and told him in French never to come near her again.

Ben went off down the street back to his hotel thinking that he must find someone like Rita, a kindly female: he was craving the kindness of women.

Richard told him that they had only three days left, and then Ben would be on his own. He did not like saying this: he did not want to leave Ben alone, and not only because it would mean the end of well-paid good times. He had become fond of this – whatever he was. He knew that Ben would be in trouble soon: he had no idea at all of what was dangerous for him and what was not.

Now Ben said that he was going back to London. He had worked out that if he had a passport, and some money, all he needed was to tell the girls at the desk to book him a flight: he had watched while other hotel guests had done this.

He wanted to see Johnston. He had done Johnston a favour. 'You just do this for me, Ben, that's right, you're doing me a bit of a favour. And I'll be real grateful to you.' These words had

had the same effect on Ben as the old lady's, 'You're a good boy, Ben.'

Ben felt warmly towards Johnston, imagined how he would be welcomed – but he was hearing Richard say, 'Ben, you don't understand, Johnston's not there now.'

'Why not? Where is he?'

'He's gone away. He's not doing the minicabs any more.'

This would be true very soon, even if not true at this moment. Johnston had said, 'I don't want him back here. And I'm not going to be here long anyway. And Rita's left. Tell him that. Tell him Rita's gone.'

Richard told Ben, and saw what he knew was unhappiness, or at least unease.

A dread was seizing Ben, a cold pain. He had had one refuge, one real friend – Rita. She was gone.

Then he remembered the old woman. He could go back to her. He had some money now and so he would be welcome, could even give her money to buy food.

He told Richard he would go to another friend, Mrs Biggs. And he found in his wallet the bit of paper she had given him. 'See,' he said. 'That's where she lives.'

'If there was a telephone number you could ring her.'

'She has a telephone,' said Ben. 'Everyone's got a telephone.'

Richard thought hard. If Ben went back to London, to this Mrs Biggs, then that would keep him out of Johnston's way. He told Ben to stay where he was – as usual at a café table – and he went off to ring telephone enquiries. Loving France, or rather, this coast, had made it easy for him to learn some adequate phrases of French, but he did have difficulty, persuading the French directory girl that yes, there was a Mrs Biggs, at this address and she had a telephone. At last he was talking to the English directory enquiries and there he was told there was no Mrs Biggs at this address and therefore no number. Then he asked to be put through to the number at eleven Mimosa House, and was answered by a woman who said that Mrs Biggs no longer lived there. She had died in hospital.

Richard told Ben that Mrs Biggs was dead, and Ben sat unmoving, silent, staring. He's upset, Richard knew, and tried to talk him out of it, with suggestions they should have lunch, and then walk along the front.

Richard did not know that Ben was so unhappy he would not talk, did not want to eat, could only sit there, not moving. It was an unhappiness that would never leave him now.

He was understanding that nowhere in London, nowhere in his own country, was anyone at all who would smile when they saw him. He was thinking of Mrs Biggs' room, where he had been happy, looking after her, of Rita, who had been kind, and then of his own home, but as soon as he imagined his mother, he saw, too, that scene where she had sat on the park bench and patted it so that Paul could come and sit by her. Paul, the image of that hated brother, rose up and filled his mind and brought with it thoughts of murder.

He could not bear to think of his mother.

Later, he did get up from his chair when Richard said he should, and did walk along the front, but he saw nothing, knew only that his heart was hurting most dreadfully, and that he felt so heavy he wanted to lie down there and then, on the pavement, where people passed and chattered and laughed.

He said he wanted to lie down.

Next day, Richard – he had a spare key to Ben's room – went up and found Ben curled on his bed, eyes open, but not moving.

Because Ben was in the habit of obeying Richard, he did get up because Richard said he must, and did go out to eat, and walk a little. He did not speak at all, not a word.

And now Richard was going to abandon Ben: the time had come. He was fussing and exhorting and persuading: 'You'll remember how to do this Ben? Just do what we've been doing together and you'll be all right.'

Ben did not answer.

On the morning Richard finally took his leave, he spoke to the girl at the desk, saying it was better if Ben had his money only in instalments. 'In some ways he's a bit childish,' said Richard. 'He hasn't had much experience of life.' When he said goodbye to Ben, up in his room, Ben curled on the bed, this rough and even cruel man knew he could easily cry. What did Johnston think he was doing, letting this loon, this simpleton, loose in the world?

And so Richard went out of Ben's life, to look for his little place, where he would live like a free man, not the hunted thing he had been all his life, waiting for the law to put its hand on his shoulders: perhaps his near-tears on leaving were a recognition that their situations in the world were similar. His plans did not turn out well. You may buy a nice little place for a quarter of a million, but then you have to live in it and pay for it, and you have to eat, too. And so Richard drifted back into crime. His story did not have a happy ending.

★   ★   ★

Ben sat on his bed and from behind his dark glasses stared at the square of blue in his wall. Richard had gone, and he had been with him all the time, since coming here. The old woman had gone, and Rita, and Johnston. In that world where he had been part of park benches and doorways and railway stations, a person might huddle by you all night so close you could feel the warmth coming out and warming you – and then in the morning, gone, and you would never see them again. He was feeling so loose and weightless and unbelonging he could drop through the floor or float about the room. Yet he had his place here: the room was paid for another two weeks. He could stay in hiding in this room; he could go out into the streets where he had been with Richard. And he was hungry. Richard had said he should use room service if he found the outside world difficult, but to Ben anything he had never done for himself was a trap where he could be enmeshed, and flounder. In the lobby he returned the smiles of the women behind the desk in Reception, then went to the café. He went to the café he knew best. The waiter brought him what he always had, steak, then some fruit. Richard had made him practise paying a bill, and he put down the amount the waiter told him, in English, but knew it was more than it had been ever before. He went to the market. Now, because Richard was not there, a shield between him and this noisy bright world, the sound of French hurt him, full of unknown meanings and threats. The two of them had bought fruit at the market, and there Ben pointed at grapes, at peaches, could not understand what the woman vendor said, held out his palm with money on it – and saw it all disappear. He knew from the small satisfied grin on that face, as she turned away, and how she slid the money she had got from him into her money pocket, that he had been cheated. He felt eyes on him; knew people commented; he sat, as he would have done with Richard at a café table to watch the events and people – and knew he would have to go through the ritual of ordering fruit juice, of paying for it – and he got up and stumbled back to the hotel. He was in a panic. It was his worst moment. The knowledge of his aloneness was beating into him, *You are alone, you are alone*. He felt danger everywhere and he was right. He had been protected by Richard, and now he was not.

He returned to his room. That night he went off into the poorer parts of the town, looking for a girl, but did not see one. He planned to try again the next night. He was thinking of Rita, for now he could remember only kindness, but before he could begin a life of wandering up and down this coast, following the smiles of whores, risking all kinds of bad trouble, something else happened.

A film-maker from New York stood at the reception desk, chatting to the two young women who were arranging a return flight to New York for him. Alex was middle-aged, but in the American way, looking youngish, lean, healthy, and with young clothes, bright and expensive. Going back home would be a defeat. After long anxieties and crises, he had made a film, three years ago, not the one he wanted to make, but he had not been able to attract the money for that. His film was about youths becoming criminals and drug dealers in a South American city, and had earned him enough attention for him to know his second film would be watched for. This time he would stand out for the film he wanted, and if it took time . . . But it was taking time, and money was getting short. For a year he had been possessed, a mad man, with one thought: which film, which story? Ideas whirled about in his mind, and even his dreams, took him to this city or country and that, possessed him totally, but left him – not good enough; and then another idea took over. He had got to the point where everyone he saw, every street, or bar or railway station or airport suggested a film. The world had become a phantasmagoria of film sets, and he knew he was a little crazy. For half a year he had believed he would make a film about the great days of a Mediterranean port in an earlier time, and that was why he was here. But nothing seemed to crystallise his ideas, and he should leave. Yet he did not want to leave this coast, and his dreams of it . . . Into the lobby from the lift came Ben, and Alex's eyes followed him. Ben went to the revolving doors out to the street, stopped, came back, and sank into a chair. He was grinning – perhaps at an attractive private thought? Alex, who had not for months been able to look at anything or anybody without his mind filling with bright seductive scenes, saw a sombre hillside under a low louring sky, with black rocks clambering and piling up it, ancient vigorous trees; he heard water splashing and from beside a little waterfall emerged a creature, squat, hairy, with powerful shoulders and a deep chest, which lifted gleaming hostile eyes to see this alien, Alex, and barked, at which from behind rocks and through trees came a company of similar creatures, and they went running up the hillside into the mouth of a cave, a big hole in the hillside, and there they assembled and stood alert, to see what threat this unknown might mean. Below them were the crowns of the old trees, of a kind Alex could have sworn he had never seen, and all around jagged rocks. This band of *what* – dwarfs? Yetis? – nothing that Alex had seen in pictures or on film

78

– held their ground there, staring at him. The tallest were five feet three or four inches, and others were shorter – females, perhaps? Hard to tell what was their sex with that hair falling from their loins. Coarse pale hair on their shoulders, beards, green eyes. Now in their hands were clubs, stones, some as sharp as knives . . . And the vision faded, it went, and Alex was staring at Ben in his smart clothes, who was looking at the revolving doors, and thinking that, yes, he would go back to London, and look for Rita, after all, there was that money for him in the safe. But Johnston would . . . It was the thought of Johnston that made that grin of fear appear again on his face. Ben had realised that Johnston had lied to him, tricked him, and now had left him helpless here, surrounded by people who made sounds he could not understand.

Alex turned back to the young women behind the desk, who were waiting for his questions about Ben: they were used to these questions. They had evolved their own ideas about Ben. One said that he had been in a mental hospital, he was a rich person, and had been sent here with a minder. Another said he was obviously a heavyweight wrestler. A third believed some experiment had gone wrong in a laboratory, and said Ben gave her the creeps. All were protective of Ben, helped him with advice, in English, and with gifts of their time, going with him to his room to make sure he had a bowl for his fruit, or to find something – once, his passport, which for a frightful morning he had thought he had lost. That passport now seemed all that stood between him and being nothing – without it who would know that he was Ben Lovatt, from Scotland, thirty-five years old, a film actor? Now these smiling helpful faces were concealing a determination to shield Ben from this film director. Dubious and even cruel exploitations were imminent, for they knew Ben to be helpless. When Alex asked, 'Who is he?' one said, 'He's from London,' and another, 'He's on holiday here.' But there was the third person, who did not believe Ben was in films, and who didn't like Alex, and she said, 'He's in films.'

Alex said, 'Forget that booking. I'll stay around a bit.' He went over to Ben, sat down, introduced himself.

Ben's grin held, and his eyes darted about, in fear, but then Alex's friendly ease reminded him of Richard and even of the old woman, and the terrified grin went, and his smile came. Alex took Ben out for a meal, and then to a café, and so that all went on for a day, and then another, and then a week, and all this time Alex, with that vision or dream in his mind of the dwarfs, or whatever they were, was thinking that he would make a film with Ben. But he did not have a story, and above all, no money either. Ideas for stories came and went, each one taking over his imagination for the time they stayed. He was possessed by those creatures – *who? – what?* – not beasts, for Ben inhabited the forms of everyday life, used a knife and fork, went every day to have his beard clipped and his hair done, changed his clothes – which were beginning to look a little shabby. Alex heard that Johnston had had shirts and jackets made specially for him. Who was Johnston? Ben said that he had cars and drivers and sent people off in them all over London but that he had gone away. Ben was vague about everything. The boundaries of his understanding were narrow enough, and his sympathies and antipathies made even stranger patterns. He talked about the old woman, but not about the cat, about Johnston, but not about Rita, because thinking of her made him so sad. He said he had a family but his father hated him and he did not mention Paul, or his mother. What Alex Beyle got out of all this was only that Ben came to him without strings. He could use him without people coming for explanations or to demand – well, what? He wasn't going to exploit Ben! He would pay him. He would look after him. Again Ben got specially made shirts and two jackets, a warm one and a thin one and some high-necked T-shirts, in silk, to hide that hairy throat and neck.

Ben knew that this friend, who was going to look after him, wanted to make a film with him in it: he really was a film actor. He did not like films, they filled his eyes with light, and made him sick. Alex took him to a cinema, a film carefully chosen, as for a child, a good strong story, excitement, danger. But Ben sat with his eyes closed, opening them in quick desperate attempts to see, but he could not see, the clashing invading light was too much for him.

Alex took Ben to an oculist to get glasses: he was sure the dark glasses were wrongly prescribed. Ben preferred the dusk of evening to light, never sat in the sun, and his eyes were often squeezed up, or squinting. This oculist too seemed nervous. When he emerged from the testing room to speak to Alex, for he had failed to communicate with Ben, he said that these were unusual eyes. They did not adapt well to changes of light. The oculist's ideas about Ben were nearest to the girl at Reception who said he was a failed laboratory experiment, but he wasn't going to say so, and get himself into trouble. He said the dark glasses Ben had were probably as good as any others might be, but suggested glasses tinted less dramatically than the very dark ones. Ben's eyes were watering badly; he was grinning – with embarrassment, the oculist thought, but by now Alex knew what that staring grin meant.

When Alex heard that Ben's hotel was paid for, for another week, and heard about the money in the safe, he was relieved. Every little helped. He had to get money for development from somewhere. He spent hours on the telephone to Los Angeles, New York, other places where films were bred, and finally persuaded the producer who financed his last film to give him enough. He did not have one story: he had several. When he described Ben there was enough of bafflement, of wonder, of excitement in his voice to extract that development money.

And now Alex had to find his story. The trouble was nothing that appeared in his mind as film matched in seductive strangeness that vision of the band of creatures in the cave mouth, looking across chasms of time – millions of years? – into the face of Alex, their – he supposed – descendant. If he was. Did their genes linger in his body somewhere? Did Ben and he share genes? Sometimes he thought that of course, yes, but there were moments when he understood how alien Ben was to him. Alex was saying quietly to himself that Ben was not human, even if most of the time he behaved like one. And he was not animal. He was a throwback of some kind. If the company of ancient men were only a kind of animal how was it that Ben could live the life of human beings – well, for most of the time?

What made Alex uneasy was that when the film was made, when all that was over, there would be Ben, and he needed looking after. For the time being it was all right. Ben spent his days with Alex and part of his evenings. Alex had friends along the coast, and in the little towns up in the hills and he did try to take Ben on visits, but it was difficult and strained and he did not try again. And what did Ben do, on the evenings when he was abandoned by Alex? He went into the town carefully, as if hunting or stalking, to look for a female. He did find one, but again was called *bête* and *cochon*, but he knew only that he was being rejected.

And now Alex had an idea. He would go back to South America to make his film. This time, Brazil. He knew people there, had even made a little film, had directed a play. He would set his story not in Northern Europe, with its association of dwarfs and gnomes and trolls, and brownies, and – more delicately, fairies and elves – he would jettison all that cargo, and go south, into forests where . . . But he had not worked it out, no tale lingered in his mind. He would go to Rio, and take Ben out into those forests where butterflies the size of thrushes flew about and where the history was as ancient and savage as in Europe – and then he would let what visions come into his mind that would.

He described South America to Ben, described Brazil, and Rio. As always he did not know what Ben understood. He got into the habit of watching for that grin that said so much. Ben asked if they were going on an aeroplane, and said he had been on a plane, a little one. He described looking down on London. He had seen where the old woman lived and the street where Johnston worked – where he had worked but he had gone away. He did not mention the plane from London to the South of France because he could not be persuaded he had been on it. Was Brazil far away, he asked? Far away from where? Alex wanted to know, but did not ask. He was feeling guilty about what he was doing. Well, he promised himself, he would see that Ben came back, either to here, or to London, where his friends would care for him.

And so Ben took what remained of the packet of money, and the two of them flew off to Rio de Janeiro.

But that was not as easy as that sounds. First, they had to take a plane to Frankfurt, for a connection to Rio. Ben stood in a line of people, Alex just in front of him, with his passport in one hand, his holdall in the other. Outside the Mediterranean sun dazzled off panes, cars, leaves, clouds. But Ben had his eyes half shut, even though he wore dark glasses, and he was grinning. Perhaps I am going home? he thought, as he stood at the check-in desk with Alex beside him saying that Ben wanted a window seat. When they got on to the plane this time he knew it was one, and in the window seat, with Alex beside him, he was able to match what he saw with what he had looked down on from the tiny plane in London. Then cloud enveloped the plane and he was looking down on a white that shone and hurt. He shut his eyes, leaned back and Alex said, 'It's only an hour, Ben.' Meaning, to Frankfurt, but there it all happened again, the crowds, the escalators, the strong lights, walking along corridors and then waiting at the gate, his boarding card in his hand. He shuffled along beside Alex, grinning.

Alex watched this despondent fellow and felt doubt, real apprehension. He would have clapped him mightily on the shoulder – 'It's OK, Ben, you'll see' – but yesterday, giving him a friendly clout, as he would have done a male friend, in America, he saw those green eyes convulse, boil and rage, and those fists . . . Alex did not know how near he had come then to being crushed in those great arms, with those teeth in his neck. He did know it was a dangerous moment, though.

Ben's rage had blanked out his vision with red, and his fists had filled with murder – he had only just subdued this dangerousness, only just held himself in. He must not ever let that rage loose, he knew it, but when Alex hit him like that . . . the unhappiness that had been deepening in him since he knew that the old woman had gone, and Johnston and Rita too, had rage as its partner. He scarcely knew whether he wanted to bellow and howl with pain, or to go berserk and kill.

There were long winding descending corridors and then the door to the interior of the plane: Ben found it hard to believe this was a plane: it was so big. He could hardly see how big. And he understood that he was not going home, but somewhere in that mind of his that was always wrestling with itself to remain in control, to understand, he was telling himself that he had been promised he would go home, and that he had been betrayed and that Alex was part of this betrayal. Brazil. What was Brazil? Why did he have to go there? Why should he be in a film?

This time he did not look out of the window, because he knew he would see only white cloud and a painful dazzle. Eleven hours flying – what would Ben do for that long cramped time? They were flying economy: Alex could not afford to waste money.

Around came the drinks. Alex told Ben he must drink some water, and Ben drank. Should Ben be given sleeping pills? But perhaps his metabolism was not amenable to drugs: like a cat given human painkillers or sleeping pills, he might be harmed, or even die. But the problem was solved, for Ben went to sleep again, clutching tight to his seatbelt, which he hated. The violent tensions in his body were too much, he could not bear them, and when he woke during the trip to stare and look around him he soon fell back into sleep.

In Rio it was morning and the light had a brazen violence that woke Ben. He was clutching his genitals and trying to struggle up. Alex got him to the lavatory in time. He was thinking, this is like looking after a child – he did have one, a son, from a marriage ended by divorce.

The hotel was no problem. Ben understood what it was, and stood in front of the reception desk with confidence. Then – and Alex saw what was happening and was angry with himself – it was a new language, it was Portuguese, and Ben had become accustomed to at least the sounds of French.

'What is it?' he asked Alex, rough, sorrowful, angry. 'What are they saying?'

Alex explained. He had spent a lot of time telling Ben about Brazil, about Rio, how beautiful; about forests, beaches, the sea everywhere, but he had not thought to say that people would be talking Portuguese.

Alex would have liked a room to himself, but he had been afraid to let Ben loose in the mysteries of this new hotel, so they were sharing a room. Only for one night: it is not difficult to rent a flat in Rio, and the next day they would move into one.

Alex was desperate to sleep, having stayed awake on the plane to keep an eye on Ben, but knew he must remain awake, for now Ben who had slept and was fresh was moving about this room like an animal taking the measure of a new place, trying the bathroom – the shower, the lavatory – opening and shutting cupboards and drawers. They were high up in the hotel, and Ben looked out and down and did not seem upset, although he had not liked the lift. He lay down on his bed and got up again, while Alex watched, in a daze of jet lag.

'I'm hungry,' said Ben.

Room service brought steaks and Ben ate Alex's as well as his. This was a country of wonderful fruit, and Alex ordered some. Ben grunted with pleasure over the pineapple but got the juice all over himself. Alex was impressed that he took himself off to the shower, without being told, and there he stayed a long time. Alex listened to sounds – what were they? Was that singing? That rough grunting chant? The water splashed about everywhere, and Alex had to mop it up.

It was still only midday.

Alex began telephoning friends. He had many in this city. Some he had worked with on the play he had done, some had been with him on the film, done in Colombia and Chile. Some were friends of friends. He had to keep awake. He knew that if he fell asleep, he would not wake until tomorrow. An early dinner was arranged. Meanwhile Alex and Ben would see the town. It was hot, light bouncing off the sea, and Ben stumbled along, clutching at Alex, his eyes almost closed. So Alex took him back again to the hotel, having elucidated from Ben that in Nice they had gone for walks in the evenings, and once, when it was cloudy, in the day. They sat at a table outside the hotel, and drank fruit juices, and Ben huddled there in his chair, not grinning – Alex was thankful to see – but so intent, his head turning this way, that way, as deep in the shade of the sun umbrella as he could get, sizing up these new people, trying to understand the new sounds. As people came and went, or sat at the other tables, just as everywhere Ben had been, they tried to comprehend what they saw. A first casual general glance taking in the scene – but left in their minds was something not assimilated, a question. A second look, much longer: well, that's just a big man, that's all – no crime to be large, to be bulky – but what shoulders, say what you like, those shoulders . . . Having turned away, a third look, surreptitious, quick. Yes, that's all it is, he's built big, but he's no beauty. And then a final open unconcealed stare, as if Ben's strangeness licensed the bad manners of staring. Yes, but *what* is it? Just *what* am I looking at? The hot afternoon went past, and Alex was being tortured by the need to sleep. Then, he couldn't stand it, and made Ben go with him back to the room. Ben did not want to go, he liked it there, watching, listening, and besides, there were females who smiled at him.

In the room Alex flung himself on the bed and was asleep. He had not even taken off his shoes.

And now Ben was on his own bed, but did not lie down. He sat on its edge and stared at Alex. He had not shared a room since the old lady, and he had not needed to examine her, or stare: the night Rita had allowed him to stay he had been too grateful to want anything but be there. But this was a male, who had brought him here, to this place, where he never asked to be. He did not like Alex, though he seemed to be kind: Ben felt that Alex had tricked him.

The defenceless man lay with his arms flung out, legs apart, face turned towards Ben, eyes so lightly closed he seemed to be watching Ben. Ben could kill him as he lay and Alex would never know it. Ben could feel the rage, fed by sorrow, strengthening in his shoulders, his arms, his fists. He could lean forward and bite hard into that throat that was presented to him there . . . But Ben knew he must not, must control himself. Even while rage darkened his eyes, another voice was telling him, 'Stop. You must not. It's dangerous. They could kill you for it.'

But Ben sat on there, letting the sorrowful rage sink down while his fists unclenched.

He was thinking of Richard: now it seemed to him that Richard had been a real friend, and that he liked him.

Ben sat a long time, legs apart, fists on his knees, leaning forward, looking. Once he held out an arm, the thick arm with big fists, and put it close to Alex's arm, that was lying loose there, so close. Alex's legs were hidden inside his jeans, but Ben knew that his own legs were like tree trunks in comparison, filling trouser legs. That face there: compared to his own it was so small and so fine; the chest visible in the carelessly closed shirt had little hair on it. They were so similar, this Alex and he, and yet so different . . . For one thing, he could crush Alex in his two arms and Alex would not be able even to move.

Ben stood at the window. It hurt to look into the glittering caverns of the sky, so he looked down. Five storeys up, they were. Not as high as the old woman. Down there people were moving about, and they were using the new language, a slushy slurry way of talking, like sugar in the mouth.

The telephone rang. Alex did not stir. It went on ringing. Ben picked up the receiver and said in English, 'Alex is asleep.' A voice, a woman's voice, said that she had heard Alex was in town and she was coming over. Alex woke. Ben said that a woman called Teresa was coming. Alex, though he was still deep in tiredness, jumped up saying, 'Oh, Teresa, wonderful, that's just great.' He showered and came back in clean clothes. It was about six. Alex took Ben down to the foyer, and there people came, more and more, until eleven of them set off to the restaurant that Alex said Ben would like, because it served mostly meat.

All of them tried to talk to Ben. Where are you from? Are you working with Alex? Have you worked on film or in the theatre? – that kind of thing, and Ben's replies silenced them because they were not to the point. For instance, asked where he was from he said, from the Excelsior Hotel in Nice, and when this friendly and curious person persisted, said he wasn't from Scotland, but didn't know the name of his home town. So they all treated Ben carefully, though kindly, trying not to stare at him. But Teresa, Ben knew, was really kind: he could feel she was.

It was the kind of restaurant they have in Rio where on the tables are already waiting plates of tomato, pickles, sauces, but it was meat that people went there for, with haunches and joints of every kind of meat, but mostly beef, displayed on platters or on skewers. Ben had never seen such a variety and amount of meat, and he was pleased, but his unhappiness was too strong for him really to enjoy himself. He felt out of things, the chattering, the embraces, the talk he did not understand, when it was in Portuguese, and even the English was mutilated and hard to follow. Soon it was over, and then he was in a car with Alex and some of the others. They were sweeping along the sea front, with the moonlight moving on the waves, and tall buildings pouring out light. At the hotel he heard arrangements being made for the days ahead: all these people were happy Alex was here, and it was as if they were expecting a holiday.

In the hotel room Ben took off his clothes, remembered to put them on hangers, and climbed, as usual, naked into bed. He watched Alex putting on pyjamas: clothes to go to bed in. Like his parents. Like himself when he was very small, but he had hated them. He fell asleep.

Now Alex did what Ben had, earlier. He sat on his bed's edge and bent forward to stare. He even held out an arm, as Ben had, and pulled up his pyjama leg to match it with Ben's, that lay outside the bedclothes, because it was so hot. Ben had a sheet pulled across his middle. Alex thought, So he has an instinct to hide his private parts – that's strange for an animal. But he's not an animal. But if he is not an animal then . . . This soliloquy seemed in danger of repeating itself, as it did, far too often, in Alex's head – and in most people's.

Alex slept. Ben slept. In the morning they ate fruit and more fruit at the hotel breakfast, and then they took their things and went to the flat Alex had rented, in a street not far from the sea front. In the lift Alex explained their flat was on 3 – not too high up: Ben still didn't like lifts. Two good-sized rooms, bedrooms, separated by a larger room that was the sitting room. A kitchen, not large; bathroom with shower and lavatory. Ben was to have his own room. Alex thought this was possibly dangerous, but he needed a room to himself: for one thing, he had a girlfriend here, Teresa. This was the first room Ben had had to himself since he had been at home with his family, and he was instinctively looking for bars in the windows: no bars. But he was feeling confined: kept testing the door – yes, he could go out and come back, he had a key. This was no trap . . . But this room, with its single bed, the big windows, was like the room he had when he was a child. It was midday. Alex said he was jet-lagged and Ben thought this meant Alex was ill: he himself did not remember being ill. Alex went to his room, saying there would be a lot of people coming around later, and that when he woke he would take Ben out and they would buy food to prepare in the kitchen. Ben was restless in his room . . . looked down into the street from where he could just hear voices talking that slushy language . . . looked across at windows opposite, where he could see people moving about there, but not know what they did. He went to the sitting room. There were some magazines there, but pictures and photographs were always of kinds of people that were not his friends, and he knew could never be. I want to go home, he was repeating, silently, in his head. Home, home.

To test if he was a prisoner he let himself out, managed to remain calm in the old, noisy lift, walked to the end of the street and back. Not many people in this side street. They all looked at him, and one followed, a young boy with a sharp angry face. Ben did not run – he knew better, but returned fast to the building where his room and safety were, and waited at the lift knowing the boy was creeping in behind him, staring, in a crouch Ben understood very well. *He must not turn and grip that boy by the shoulders . . .* The lift rattled down as the boy had almost reached him – what did he want? – and Ben was in the lift, and then fitting his key into the flat door, which opened, and Alex was there. 'Oh, there you are . . . I was wondering . . .' Alex smiled, but Ben knew he had not liked finding Ben gone. Then Alex asked if he wanted to go back to the pavement outside the hotel where the tables were, and Ben said yes, he would. They sat there eating sandwiches and drinking juice, watching people of all colours, black and brown and pale brown and white, go wandering past. A lot of girls, some of them with hardly any clothes on. There were girls at these tables, sometimes in pairs, or by themselves. Ben could not stop himself watching them, and wanting. He was thinking of Rita, and how she liked him. Alex told him to be careful, because the girls usually had men who protected them. 'Like Johnston,' Ben said, adding another ingredient to Alex's view of this Johnston. 'Did he take her money?' he asked. 'She never asked me for money,' said Ben. 'She liked me.' 'I think you'd find these girls would ask for quite a lot of money.'

All that went along well, sitting there under the umbrellas, watching the people, Alex sometimes greeting friends, and then Alex bought food, and Ben helped him carry it all back to their place. Alex cooked, and Ben said he could help, he knew how to cook – but he was thinking of the toast and porridge and bits of this and that he had made for the old lady, and soon saw this was more difficult cooking. Ben sat in the living room, smelling the aromas of spices and hot meat, and then in came a lot of people, and he watched them all kissing and hugging and holding each other; and talking and chattering, their teeth flashing and gleaming. The light had gone outside. This was a different night from the ones in Nice: it was hot, and slow, with sometimes a strong smell of sea. Some of these people were the same as last night's, but to each newcomer Alex said, 'This is Ben, we are going to make a film together.' And as they said, '*Como vai?*', 'Welcome', 'Hello', each gave him the surprised curious look he knew, and then they were careful not to look, or he caught them staring, hoping he wouldn't notice. The food came in, piled on platters, a lot of it, and wine was in every glass and bottles of wine stood about the room. There was such a noise, such a clamour of voices, and Ben did not understand much of what was said, even when they spoke English. There were plans being made, and he was in them. The talk, the eating, the drinking, went on till late.

Ben slept lightly in that room which made him think of his old home, and woke early. He did not dare go out into the street for fear of another killer boy, stalking him. He ate fruit, he stood at windows looking out. Alex did not get up till late, and when he came into the sitting room Teresa was with him: Ben had failed to notice that this female had gone with Alex into his room last night.

But she was friendly, and helpful, making food for him, offering him juice, and when he sat silent and doleful included him in what she said, in her quick, but difficult English. 'What do you think about it, Ben?' 'Would you like that, Ben?' 'What do you want me to get you?' He liked her very much, but knew she belonged to Alex.

And so the days went, slowly, and Ben slept a lot, from boredom. The evenings were full of people, who arrived loudly, laughing and talking to each other in Portuguese but to Alex and Ben in their hard-to-understand English. They sometimes brought food, not always. Ben sat apart and watched. He was trying to understand why when they were all so different, they could so easily be together, as if they did not know how different they were. Mostly they had smooth darkish skins, and dark eyes, contrasting with Alex, who was pale, a thin, thin-boned man, with pale hair, and his clothes were pale blue, trousers and shirts, or white. Over the eyes were brushes of short fair hair, but the face said Alex was not as young as he wanted to seem: the eyes had wrinkles under them. He was forty, five years more than Ben's passport said he was. No one who came to this place was as young as Ben really was, eighteen. Though that was confusing to think about: he knew he did not look like one of *their* eighteen-year-olds: he did not have that young face. Yet whenever he thought about his age, how he was, he remembered the old woman's, 'You're a good boy, Ben.'

Teresa was a tall young woman, with a big bottom and big breasts, but her waist was small, clinched with a belt to show it off. She had black hair, loose to her shoulders. Her eyes were dark. She was always smiling, laughing, and her voice was soft and easy on Ben's feelings. She put her arms around Alex, around people who came in, and, too, around Ben. 'Dear Ben,' she said often, hugging him, making him want to do what he knew he must not. But no one else touched him. Only Teresa came inside the distance all the others set between them and him. Only Teresa would take his hand, swing it, drop it; squeeze his big shoulders and say, 'Oh, your shoulders, what shoulders, Ben,' or put her arm around him as she stood talking to someone.

A man who came often was Paulo, who had worked with Alex before. They were writing a script for this film about Ben, but not always in the flat. The two might sit for a while at the table in the sitting room, talking, not looking at Ben, while Teresa tidied up the place, or cooked something, or sat on a chair-arm swinging her legs, watching the men, or reading the magazines, or sometimes singing. Then the men went out and Ben knew it was because they found his presence there wrong for what they were doing, or thinking. He knew that the story was changing all the time, because Brazil was not like the north: Ben knew

95

now he had come from the north. Paulo was different in every way from Alex, being large, with soft brown flesh, big brown eyes, dark hair, and little fat hands with rings on them. Paulo wanted to please Alex, Ben knew: they all did. Alex was the one they all turned to, watched; they waited to hear what he thought.

Sometimes on those evenings there were as many as fifteen or twenty people for supper. Every day Alex bought a lot of food, and Teresa and he cooked it. Ben heard Teresa arguing with Alex about feeding so many people, some of them he did not even know, but they came because they knew there would be food. He always said, 'Sure, come in, sit down, what'll you drink, you're welcome.'

'You talk like my wife, Teresa, now shut up,' said Alex.

When he had been here before, working on the play, he had a flat like this one, and the cast and their friends spent free time with him and he fed them. This happens with Americans, or, for that matter, with anyone who has more money than others, who are often poor, like most of the people who came to this flat, actors, dancers, singers in work or out of it, and it was natural for Alex to feed them, and often find reasons to give them money – asking them to advise him, translate something, show him a possible site, take him to a museum.

But the development money was not a great amount; Alex had had more last time he was here, working on the film or on the play. Teresa knew how much there was, and that it was going fast. And still there was no script, although Paulo and Alex worked on it every day.

There was a story, but not much of one. In a wild and beautiful part of Brazil, in foothills beneath great mountains, lived a tribe of people like Ben. They fed themselves from the forests on fruits and vegetables, hunted game with clubs and bows and arrows, and knew fire – in fact, in the course of the film they would see lightning strike a tree and make a fire.

The trouble was, apart from the discovery of fire there wasn't much going on, once you had grasped the basics: caves, the hunt, mating, gathering plants. Ben listened to all this and knew it was wrong, but not how or why: they didn't ask what he thought. Sometimes Alex and Paulo would lift their gaze from a worried inspection of their notes, scribbled over sheets of paper, their by now many drafts, outlines, developments, and, not knowing they were doing it, stare deeply at Ben, frowning, but not seeing him.

Well, how were they going to go on? Perhaps into this on the whole pleasant scene would come a tribe of more advanced people, and . . . what? The two races would mate and make a new one? The newcomers could kill out Ben's people, and Ben with them, who would die a hero defending them? Perhaps better if Ben's people killed all the newcomers, postponing an inevitable fate, for everywhere over this land were spreading the new people. No trouble about casting these. They would be the native Indians of the area. What area, though? A trip must be made, locations determined, and discussions begun with a sympathetic tribe who would be pleased to get some money: about that they need have no doubt at all.

The area they had decided on, Paulo advising, the hills of Matto Grosso, was meanwhile afflicted with bad weather, storms and flooding. The reconnaissance trip was postponed for a week, and during that time discussions went on about taking Ben to a certain town on a regular plane service, and then on from there, in a privately chartered little plane. Alex and Paulo took it for granted that they must have Ben. He heard the two men talking, in the next room, and the miserable anger that already had him in its grip deepened. Where were they going to take him? Yet again he was going to leave behind a familiar place, and get into a plane and then into another. New places, perhaps another language.

He asked Teresa when they were going to take him away and she said it would be soon. She was arguing with Alex that it would be cruel to take Ben. Couldn't he see how unhappy Ben was?

One evening, when it was late and guests were thinking of leaving, they heard a regular thud, thud, thud from next door – from Ben's room. They had not noticed he had quietly left the company, all talking about the hills and mountains of where the film-makers intended to be. Teresa quietly opened his door, and saw that he was squatting on the floor, his fists supporting him, and he was banging his head on the wall, thud, thud, thud. Teresa shut the door, came back and told what she had seen.

'Kids do that,' said Alex. 'A neighbour's kid did that. He banged his head against the wall, sometimes for hours. The doctor said it was OK, it wouldn't hurt him.'

Teresa said, 'He doesn't want to go. He's frightened.'

The company was silent, listening: thud, thud, thud.

'It'll scramble his brains,' said someone.

'No, no,' said Alex, 'leave him, it's all right.'

The guests left. Alex and Teresa sat on, listening. It was disturbing. Teresa's eyes were full of tears. Her heart hurt her, listening. On it went, the banging. She went back into Ben's room. He was whimpering as he banged his head, a small child's whimper, and Teresa put her arms around him, kneeling beside him, and said, 'Ben, dear Ben, poor Ben, it's all right, I'm here.' He gave a big shout of pain and anger and turned to her, and she felt that hairy face on her bare upper chest, and knew that this was a child she was holding, or at least a child's misery. 'Ben, it's all right. You don't have to go anywhere. I promise you.'

She stayed there beside him, on the floor, holding him, while he whimpered himself into stillness. Alex, concerned for her, peered in, withdrew. Then Ben was quiet, and Teresa got him up and on to his bed. She came out to Alex and challenged him with defiant tear-filled eyes and said, 'You can't take him. I've promised him. You cannot do it.'

'Well, I suppose we don't really need him,' said Alex.

But it was still raining in the hills where they were expected, and every evening the people sitting around the table eating, drinking, arguing, laughing, heard from next door, on the wall that separated this room from Ben's, the thud thudding of his pain, his rage.

His anger was threatening to come roaring up out of him and into his fists; he wanted to hit and to bite and to destroy – mostly Alex. Ben did not believe Teresa when she said Alex would leave him here: he was tricking Teresa, just as he had tricked him, Ben, to bring him here.

That thudding: it was awful, it spoke direct to the nerves of anyone listening, it was not possible to ignore it. They all tried to but their talk stopped, and became a listening. Alex would say, 'Take no notice; he's not harming himself.' So the talk began again, rose in a crescendo, in opposition to the thudding, but all those faces showed apprehension, irritation, even fear, and soon they were silent again, their glasses resting in their hands, their food ignored on their plates. Bang, bang, bang, on the wall.

'He must be hurting his brain,' Paulo protested, but Alex said again, 'No, kids do it, it means nothing.'

But the truth was, that nightly bang-banging was telling Alex that the vision that had been inhabiting his imagination in the hotel in Nice, was not enough to carry this film on through its many stages, the inevitable difficulties, crises, contingencies. And he still had to get together a script, or at least a detailed outline, which would extract more money, enough to actually make it.

Alex and Paulo decided to fly off, although the rain was still falling in the hills where everyone agreed they would find the landscapes they wanted. They were to leave on a Monday, and on Sunday, from midday onwards the convivial communal room was full of people. The film-makers would be gone at least a week. In this hospitable flat would remain Ben and Teresa, who would look after him.

Ben could hear the talk, talk, talking about the arrangements, and he was walking about the room as if in a cage. He came out of his room and stood looking at them all. They did not see him there. They were all a bit drunk, affectionate with each other, noisy. Teresa had her arm around Alex, and her black hair was falling on his neck. Ben went to the door and let himself out. It was late afternoon, the light slanting and radiant, but not as bad as the midday glare. He did not know what he meant to do. He walked down to where the sea showed as a blue dazzle. His eyes were hurting inside his dark glasses, but not too much. Then, in front of him, was the long white beach and on it so many people lying or playing. Jumping about among the waves were more. The girls were wearing so little he had to look to determine: yes, there was a patch of covering there in front, and those little scraps of stuff hid nipples. He was energized with anger, the need to hurt, to kill. He was walking along the top part of the beach, trying not to let the splinters of light get into his eyes, listening to the noise of waves, voices, laughter – that mass of people, so many people, who knew how to be together, all the same as each other even though they were of different colours, sizes, shapes – no one stared at them for their strangeness.

That beach, like the other beaches of Rio, was worked by gangs of thieves, mostly children or youths, and they had targeted Ben from when he came down out of the street to the sea's edge. They have a trick that goes like this. A youth, or even a child, darts up to the victim and squirts on to his shoes blobs of grease, which perhaps he, or she, does not notice at first. Then suddenly there is a disgusting slug of pale fat on one shoe or both. Ben let out a shout of fury. The tricksters, for they work in teams, are running along parallel to the victim, are waiting for the moment he sees the grease and exactly then, one runs up and offers to wipe the shoe or shoes clean, stating his price. Ben had no money on him, and anyway he was crazy with rage. He took the grinning youth, who bent towards his feet with the cleaning rag, into his arms and began squeezing him, while he – not the youth, who had no breath in him – roared and shouted with rage. Instantly the rest of the gang came crowding up to rescue their colleague, and a strolling observer – the police – took note and came running. Ben was now intermittently visible, an arm, a leg, his head, inside a knot of struggling half-naked boys.

Alex and Teresa, followed by their friends, were running towards the scene, which had silenced that part of the beach.

Teresa was shouting, in Portuguese, to the policeman, 'Stop, make them stop, he's with us!'

Who was? Ben was hardly to be seen; bellows and roars came from under the heap of assailants.

The policeman began hitting a head, arms, a leg, whatever emerged, and grabbed some youth upwards by the hair. There was a shout that the police were there, and at once the heap of youths detached themselves and darted away, some of them bloody, one with an arm that looked broken. Ben was crouching, his arms protecting his head. His clothes had been torn almost off him. His shirt was in the hand of an escaping youth, and his sullied shoes had disappeared.

Teresa began on a sharp but pleading argument with the policeman. 'He's with us – he's with him . . .' indicating Alex. 'We're making a film. It's for television.' This inspired plea made the policeman retreat, to stand a few paces off. He was staring at Ben, those hairy shoulders, that bushy face where the white teeth grinned painfully.

Teresa put her arm around Ben, whose great chest was heaving, and who was letting out grunts which Teresa knew would probably become whimpers which must – she knew – provoke a reaction in this policeman whose face would cease to be scandalised, worried, and become cruel.

'Come on, Ben,' she said, walking him away. Alex was on Ben's other side, but Ben did not look at him, only at Teresa, his poor face, where blood was trickling, a plea for her to save him.

The policeman stood staring, but let them go off, the three in front, Alex, Ben and Teresa, the rest behind.

In the flat people were still sitting around the table, hardly aware that Ben had gone and the others after him. They had never seen Ben in anything but clean clothes, smart clothes, and now they were shocked at what they saw.

Teresa took Ben to the bathroom and – as the old woman had done – took off what remained of his clothes, without embarrassment, talking gently to him. 'It's all right, you're safe now, don't be frightened, poor Ben, stand in the shower, that's right.' And Teresa washed off the sand and dirt, stopped the blood from a scratch on his forehead, and put his torn trousers into the washing machine. She fetched clean clothes, dressed him, and he let her do all this, passive in her hands, turning around when she asked, lifting an arm or a foot.

He was shocked, breathing badly, pale, and his eyes had in them a dark, lost look.

She sat with him on his bed, rocking him, 'It's all right, Ben. I'm your friend. It's all right, you'll see.'

That night which because of Alex leaving the next day she should have spent with him in his bed, Teresa was with Ben, who was lying dressed on his bed, not sleeping. She was holding his hand and talking softly to him. She was worried by his passivity, his indifference. This young woman who had seen everything in her short life of extremes of all kinds, knew very well that this Ben, the unknown, was in a crisis, was undergoing some kind of inner change.

In the morning the two men went off to the airport, and Teresa was left in the flat with Ben, and enough money to feed them both. Ben's own money was still mostly unspent.

And now Ben came out of his room, and did what he had not before: he sat down at the big table, instead of in a chair at the side of the room, out of the way. He sat there looking around the empty room and watched Teresa tidying and cleaning and obediently ate what she cooked for them both.

He had indeed changed. There had been something about that scene at the sea's edge, the deliberate deception of the youths, and then the attack, and how he was helpless under it in spite of his great strength – there were so many of them, and they were using on him holds and pressures that had immobilised him – his rage had disappeared, leaving him sorrowful because of his knowledge of his physical helplessness during those few moments – perhaps three minutes, even less. Always, until then, he had kept with him a knowledge of that strength of his, and that he did have some resort; a last defence, and he was not entirely at the mercy of others. But he had been helpless, and there had been cruelty, viciousness, the intention to hurt him.

He said to Teresa, 'When am I going home?'

Teresa knew that he had been in London, and that probably was what he meant, but she said cautiously only that she was sure Alex would take him home.

'I want to go home,' said Ben, 'I want to go home now.'

When Teresa had finished tidying and cooking she brought Ben fruit juice and sat beside him, with her glass of juice. He hoped that she would put her arm around his shoulders so that her soft black hair would fall on him, and she did. 'Poor Ben,' she said. 'Poor Ben. I am sad for you.'

'I want to go home.'

Teresa wanted to go home too, and, like Ben, hardly knew where the place was she could rightfully call home.

★   ★   ★

This was her story. She had been born in a poor village in the north-east of Brazil where now drought was killing animals and filling the fields with dust. She remembered dryness and hunger and watching their neighbours leave for the south, for Rio, São Paulo. Then her father said they must leave, they would all die if they stayed: father, mother, and four children, the eldest Teresa. For part of the way they were on a bus, but then it was a question of a bus or eating. They walked for days, eating bread and stolen maize from fields which were getting greener as they went south. Then they were in a crowded favela outside Rio, where houses were built one above another up a hillside, and where the higher you were the better, because of how sewage washed downhill when it rained. With their last money they made a shelter of plastic sheets on sticks, and below them were shacks like theirs and better houses, between paths that were becoming the sharp gashes of erosion. There was no money left. The father, together with the other poor men, tried to get work, fought for any work at all, and sometimes did get work for a day or two. They were hungry, they were desperate. Then something began which Teresa did not at first understand, though she did know the girls from the favelas earned money with their bodies. Her father said nothing, her mother said nothing, but she could read their faces, which said that she could feed this family of six people. Teresa spoke to the girls who were already feeding their families. They hung around the barracks where soldiers came out at evenings, or went to cafés where the petty criminals were. Most of these girls took it for granted they were low, they were rubbish, and that they could hope for nothing better. To get higher meant money for a good dress and shoes, and the moment there was money in their hands it went to their families. Teresa was a clever girl, clear-sighted, and she had no intention of remaining a soldiers' whore. At the start she went with another girl, to see how things went, and easily attracted a soldier who took her standing against a wall, and gave her enough *reais* to buy food for a couple of days. Teresa was sick with terror of disease, and with fear that she would never get out of this life. She went with soldiers for as long as it was needed to save enough money for a dress and shoes, while giving her mother the rest. 'Is that all?' her mother said, taking the *reais* from her: her voice was rough, her eyes ashamed, and she scolded Teresa all the time, though they had been friends. The inhabitants of the favelas, when they watched the girls go out at dusk, made angry remarks, and the men would come after them as they returned, trying to force them to give them sex for free.

Teresa had been a good girl who went to church; the priest and the teacher in school liked her and told her parents this daughter of theirs was a gift from God. She had become someone people shouted ugly names after. She felt ugly. For those weeks of walking from the north she had worn old jeans that had holes in them and a shirt that had been her father's. This was what she still wore, here, to entice custom and was why she could charge so little. There was no proper place to wash. Her hair was greasy. She knew she smelled bad.

She had to force herself to go into a shop as she was and buy a dress. She was afraid they would simply throw her out. She knew exactly what she wanted: she had seen the dress on a rail, from the pavement. She walked in, the money in her hand, and said, 'I want that one.' She knew she could not try it on, being so dirty. The assistant took her money, and put the dress in a bag, giving Teresa cold angry looks. 'I want you to keep it here for me – just for a few days,' said Teresa.

The assistant did not want to, but Teresa's pleading eyes did speak loudly enough to make her change her mind. She would put the bag aside, but only for a week. Teresa knew she could not take that dress into the favela: her mother would have it off her, to sell for food. And Teresa privately agreed that her mother would be right. She knew too well the anguish of watching children ask for food that wasn't there.

Teresa was stood up against a wall, in the dark, and even in day-light, until she had money for good shoes. She got the dress from the shop, and put it on, a red dress, with a cleavage, but not too much, tight at the waist – she was a different person. She did this behind a bush in a public garden. She put on the shoes, high-heeled, delicate: she was going to find it hard walking in them. And now she had to find a way to clean herself, and this needed more courage than anything she had done. She went boldly to a big hotel, one of the best, and into it, as if she belonged there. The hardest was walking in those shoes so people would think she was used to them. The employees in the hotel lobby did take a good look, but thought she was off to join some man in his room. She found a toilet, and no one else was there. She lifted up that dress and, using a rag she had brought with her, washed her legs and up to her waist; slipped the dress down and washed armpits and breasts. Tempted to take the soap away, to give her family, pride stopped her: I'm not a thief, she decided. Someone came in, hardly glanced at Teresa, used a cubicle, came out, washed her hands, standing beside Teresa who was washing her hands.

The intruder went. Now Teresa was clean, except for her hair, and she had to take her biggest risk yet. She washed her hair, unable to hear properly for that time, and was lucky enough to have her hair out of the basin, while she was standing leaning back to squeeze water out of it, when a woman came in, and stared, but did not say anything. She left. Teresa combed her wet hair. She knew that now, clean, in her new red dress, her tall white shoes, with her hair smooth and sleek she was as good as anybody, and she walked out of the hotel and sat down at a table in the sun, so that her hair would dry. It was late morning. She did not know how to judge the people there, tourists mostly, except for the girls whom she knew to be from the favelas, like herself. Like herself, they were all good-looking. With a nice dress and shoes and the price of a drink a pretty girl from one of the worst slums in the world could sit at a table outside a fine hotel and no one would say a word. A waiter might, though. The other customers might not know who they were, the waiting girls, but the waiters would have understood it all.

But when one came, she ordered an orange juice and sat there, by herself, a long time. She saw one of the girls go off with a man into the hotel. At last a man did come to sit at her table, and she had to be courageous. He was a tourist, and spoke ten words of Portuguese. He was a German. He asked how much, she told him a sum so enormous she waited for him to laugh at her: but this was a famous hotel, she knew that, and everyone here was well-dressed, and very well-fed. He said, yes, he agreed. Now she had a bad moment: was he going to ask her if she had a room? But no, he took her arm and they walked back through the town to a smaller hotel, where no one stopped him, with her, going to the lift. She was carrying with her, in the glossy bag of the dress shop, her old clothes, which did not smell nice. She managed to leave this bag in the lift, as they went out of it.

This man liked her, and asked her to come every day – he had a week here. This was a stroke of luck: she did not know yet how big a one it was. But perhaps it was not only luck. She was beautiful, she discovered, looking into the long mirror in the room. She was beautiful and she had an aptitude for sex. She did not mind him. He was not like the soldiers.

At the end of the week with the German she took her mother more money than she had ever done, at one time. But it was not all she had, and she was becoming obsessed with the danger she was in, carrying wads of money taped under her breasts. Banks were not for people like her. She did not even have an identity card yet, and knew that if the police caught her she would be in bad trouble. She stood in line for a day and got her card, a piece of paper saying she was Teresa Alves. She felt let down by this identity card, which did not match what she felt about herself. And the card did not solve her problem with the money. A certain shopkeeper would keep money for customers, for a price, but she did not trust him. Yet she had to, and did give him half of what she had.

She did not go to the tables outside that first hotel for a week, and when she did, she had bought another dress, a green one, and she had been to a real hairdresser for the first time in her life. She was by far the prettiest woman at those tables, and she got another customer at once, a Greek. Her career at that hotel went on well, for a couple of months. The family was being fed. Her nest egg was growing. And she was planning how to escape being a tart. She was less afraid than she had been, in the time of the soldiers, about disease, but she was nervous, although she had been to a doctor who told her she was all right – so far.

Being a whore was expensive. She knew that her profession was costing her, in clothes and expensive drinks and make-up and the hairdresser and paying a maid in the hotel to keep her good clothes safe for her, what her father had earned in years of his life of being a poor farmer.

Then she had another lucky break: she was lucky, she knew. One of her customers, an American working in the theatre, used her for information about local manners and mores, took her on trips to check out locations, asked her to translate simple things – by now she knew some English, not much, but enough to make it seem that she knew much more. And so she was becoming known in that world: television, film, theatre, and was offered work. And she gave up whoring, though she would earn less money being respectable. She went back to the favela every few days; she had a cheap room in Rio: at last she had a place to keep her money and her clothes. Her mother said to her with bitterness that soon she would take herself off, ungrateful daughter, and leave them all to starve. But Teresa could never do that, and her mother knew it. Both understood the mother was angry out of shame. Now Teresa told her that she had a good job, but her parents did not believe her, but pretended to, to save her face – and theirs, so they were not living off a tart's wages.

The family was better off than many in the favela. The father had built a little brick house with an iron roof, where the rain banged and thundered. There were two rooms and in them not six people, but three, mother, father, and a sickly little girl. The two boys, the one nearest to Teresa, fourteen, and the one down from him, twelve, had joined the gangs of boys that roamed the streets, stealing, taking what they could. If they did return home it was only to demand some money and they were off again. Sometimes Teresa saw a gang of street kids, looked out for her brothers and saw them rushing past, or idling with blank eyes, on the pavement edges. Drugs. They took them and they sold them. She scolded them, but knew she ought to be afraid of these cool, cruel street children who killed for the sake of a handful of *reais*. But she had helped bring them up, recently had fed them, and so she felt she had the right to scold. She gave them money. And then had to keep a lookout for the gangs, because it might not be only her brothers she could expect to come demanding money.

Two years ago Alex had employed her, when he was working on the play, and they had become lovers. She made a favour of it to begin with, did not want him to think she went with the job. But he would not have minded, or even noticed, much. He was fond of her, relied on her, and had no idea at all of the dirty roads she had travelled, at first literally, from her faraway dying village, and then, using her body to escape from poverty. He took things as they came, and in Rio there was lovely Teresa, and she was certainly not more than he deserved. He was used to the good things in life and he liked being liberal with his money. 'I have a mother,' she said. 'I give her money.' And he gave Teresa money, a good salary, more than he would have done if there had not been this mother.

When Teresa allowed herself to think about her situation she was attacked by panic. On her entirely depended her mother, her father, and the sickly child. She was scheming how to rescue her brothers. The trouble was, her room in the flat of a minor singer who let the room to keep herself eating was tiny, and she could not ask her brothers there. If she earned more, got a better place? – but she was not prepared to go back to prostitution. Responsibilities sat on her shoulders like heavy sacks she had to carry. She was seventeen, though she pretended to be twenty-two, just as she put on a show of knowing more English than she did. She often dreamed of her village, though it had been so poor and life so hard: at least she had been looked after. She yearned to have somebody between her and the dangers that surrounded her. It was her mother's strong arms she wanted, and she knew it.

And so there sat Teresa, her head on her hand, thinking of how as a child running about in the dust she had no idea that so soon she would have such a load on her, and Ben sat at the table with her, grieving, 'I want to go home.' And sometimes Teresa put her arms round him, 'Poor Ben,' and even, 'You're a good boy, Ben.' Even while she said this she reminded herself that this was a bearded man who, his passport said, was thirty-five, even if he had told her he was eighteen. People treated him as if he were younger than that, and he behaved like an obedient child, she thought. People behave as they're treated. She changed her manner towards him, asking him like an adult person to do little things for her, make her a sandwich, or coffee; she believed she saw a difference in him because of it.

He did not always sit with her. The door between the big room and his bedroom usually stood open, and she knew what he was up to. Usually he lay on his bed, or sat on it, trying out the dark glasses. In the afternoon the light came hard into his room so sometimes it seemed Ben was in a quivering pool of water. To him it seemed that splinters and needles of brightness tried to dart into his eyes, fill his head with dazzle. He tried on the glasses, pair after pair, and always ended up with the darkest of them: Richard had bought him two more pairs. Then he attempted to do without, while the white heat of the day moved about on the wall in patterns of brilliance. 'Why are my eyes so different?' he fiercely asked, addressing something that could be called Fate, Destiny – the painful emotions summoned up in him by the old lady's and Teresa's *Poor Ben*. But why, why *why* was he so different?

Meanwhile Alex and Paulo were far away in the hills, which they had reached by means of a tiny aeroplane, from a town that itself was served by a plane once a day. They had wanted to drive up into the hills but it had rained so much the roads were bad. They had landed up in a little hotel, or guest-house that Paulo remembered from a previous reconnaissance in this area which was visited by the occasional prospector, or anthropologist, or geologist. It had four rooms and was surrounded by a deep veran-dah on which the two men sat working on their script. They had tramped over a good many hills, with Ben in their minds – Ben and his people. The trouble was that while that vision of Ben's tribe he had experienced in the hotel in Nice was fresh in his imagination, so that he often referred to it, as a check, Alex more often saw Ben as he was now, a miserable angry creature who both he and Paulo believed was probably ill. Ben made Alex feel guilty, and he had times of regretting bringing Ben out to Brazil, and even the whole idea. It was not working. When things worked, and would go on well, then that is what they did: there was a momentum, everything fitted and intermeshed, people, events, an article in a magazine or a book casually picked up contributed to the process, and it was by this fortuitousness that you knew you were in a lucky streak. But with this project – this film – everything ground and bumped along, or came to a halt together. How many times had they restarted the script, believed it to be good, but then doubts began and they knew it wasn't? Alex now knew that it had been the powerful presence of Ben that had been impetus enough to carry them along. Ben as he had been. But now Ben was the block, a lock on their creative imaginations, when they thought of him what they heard was the bump, bump, thud, thud, of his head on the wall. They did joke that the sound was like that of minestamps: they could hear the stamps from a little mine near the guest-house. This joke was their attempt to bring Ben back into something congruous, that could feed their ideas.

They had not only wandered over a good many hills and minor mountains but had visited a tribe of Indians, and it was from that meeting that began the process that was – at first tacitly but now openly – removing Ben from the film.

They had gone by plane – the third, a four-seater – away over forests and rivers, and had landed in a rainforest where there were people who were not hostile, but pleased with what they had brought . . . Paulo advising. There were two small radios, with batteries – a good many of these in thick plastic bags to keep out the hot wet – tinned food, clothing, knives. Paulo had done the talking: he knew a few words of the local language, while Alex sat silent, but his eyes were hard at work. What faces! What bodies! *What* a beautiful people these were, living their still uncorrupted life on the edge of a river. It had been these people who, in an early version of their script, had invaded the territory of Ben's tribe, and then . . . but Paulo and he had been unable to decide what then.

There were pretty girls, one in particular, the most delicately beautiful creature Alex had ever seen. She was about fourteen, they were told, and would soon marry. This tribe was not averse to being in a film, but limits were imposed, one being that none of the youngsters could be taken away from here to the temptations of a big city – which, for these people, was a town an hour's plane ride from here, whose name the film-makers had trouble in finding on a map.

That girl . . . She was in both their minds; they confessed to being overwhelmed by her. They returned to their verandah, and the guest-house that was run by an elderly man and woman who asked every morning what they wanted to eat, but it always turned out to be chicken and rice and beans, and hot spices, and chicken again. They drank beer chilled in a refrigerator run on batteries, for the power up here was chancy, and it often failed. The two threw aside all their earlier versions of the script and began again, with the tribe and the girl as a starting point. It is not true to say that Ben disappeared entirely. At first this girl was being forced to marry a wild hill man who had found gold and with it wanted to buy the girl, and this man did retain some of Ben's characteristics as perceived by Alex, mainly a rough stupidity. Then the suitor lost his crudeness, and was handicapped only by a crippled leg, which the girl cured – so you could say that Ben's actuality dwindled into a gammy leg. In the end there was a film, and it did quite well. The girl became a television star and was to be seen every day on the screens in Rio. This was a kind of happy ending, and the girl certainly thought so, at least at the beginning of her career: when she was older she was not so sure.

Meanwhile Alex telephoned Teresa from a town where they had to fly to get the use of a reliable telephone. Alex said he would be here for another week or so. It was very cheap living here and they wanted to visit a certain tribe again. Please would Teresa stay in the flat, look after Ben, and prepare him for the news that he would not be in the film.

Teresa was indignant and did not conceal it. Ben should not have been treated like this – just scooped up and then dropped. She was delighted too, but concealed that: she knew Ben would be damaged even worse if they put him in a film, that is, if he could deal with it all. She was cool, discussing terms and conditions. Money was running out. Well, said Alex, she could use Ben's money, and Alex would replace it. And how was Ben? 'He's – fine,' said Teresa, telling Alex nothing, nor intending to. 'He is fine.'

'Great,' said Alex.

'Shall I tell him you will take him home soon?'

'Yeah, yeah, I told him I would. But I've been thinking, Teresa. If he likes Rio, he could stay. What do you think?'

'He wants to go home,' said Teresa, and her voice was tearful.

'Fine, fine, that's OK. Tell him we'll be back soon.'

Teresa told Ben that he would not be in the film, because she knew that would make him happy, but not that Alex would be back soon, because she knew Ben feared him.

Two weeks had gone, then three. There was a domestic routine. In the morning Teresa went out to get fresh bread, and she made coffee for herself, and poured fruit juice for Ben. She tried to make him eat more, but he had lost his appetite and was thin and wretched. Teresa loved to be on the beach, but Ben could not go there, nor be left too long by himself. She went with him, not to the hotel tables where she had achieved her step up from absolute poverty, but to another where she was not known. He wore his dark glasses, and a Panama hat she had bought him, which he pulled down low over his eyes. They sat there a couple of hours, drinking juice, and watching people. Teresa was interested in Ben's reactions: he might seem to shrink away, while his white stretched grin appeared in his beard. 'What is it, Ben?' 'He's bad,' Ben would say. 'He hurts me.' 'But I am with you, Ben.' She strained to see what in this apparently harmless person might be frightening Ben, but could not. Or his small pleased smile might appear, and she saw another equally unthreatening person – usually a woman. 'You must be careful, Ben, when you smile at girls.' 'I like her,' Ben might say. And once, 'I think she likes me?' After such excursions Teresa felt that she had survived dangers and was pleased to be back, where she made a steak to tempt him, and a sandwich for herself. In the long hot afternoons they lazed, and her friends might drop in, one or two, but in the evenings it was not unlike how it was with Paulo and Alex; but now people came in with a bottle of wine, or some meat to cook, or fruit – this place could no longer be a cornucopia of hospitality, for Teresa did not have the money for it, and would not spend Ben's, more than she had to. And Ben did not retreat to his bedroom, but stayed, and even sat on with them at the table. He was not included in the talk, which kept moving off from what he knew, but he took in what he could, which was more than Teresa or the others suspected. They all laughed a lot, but frequently he wondered what they found so funny: to him it was often frightening. More and more he remembered the old woman, her care for him, her kindness; he even thought of the cat as a companion he had lost. Ben knew Ellen Biggs had died, but that did not prevent him from thinking about her, as someone who would welcome him if he arrived at her door.

The people who came to visit Teresa were of a lower sort than Alex's guests. No film directors and script writers, no well-known actors and dancers. These were small fry, on the fringes of theatre and television, theatre technicians, PR girls, an interpreter Teresa cultivated to learn more English from. A make-up girl had taught Teresa all she knew, and from a singer in a club sailors frequented she had learned some songs and how to play the guitar. No girls from the favela, no one who could remember Teresa as she had been, and not so long ago, either. Among these people was a young woman Teresa secretly thought of as her prize. Her name was Inez, and she was the daughter of a good family: her father was a university professor and she worked as an assistant in a scientific laboratory. Teresa had met her when a short TV film was being made about genes, inheritance – all that sort of thing – and Inez's father was consulted. Inez was attracted by the theatre as only those can be whose lives have been in a groove since birth. She saw herself as doomed to predictability.

Teresa was in awe of this clever young woman who had been educated in a way that meant her talk was always astonishing Teresa with possibilities she could never have imagined. And Inez was fascinated by Teresa. Unlike Alex, who could not respond when Teresa told him she had walked hundreds of miles to reach Rio, Inez knew very well what Teresa had escaped. She had flown over the desiccating regions where the dust clouds lay so high in the air she had scarcely been able to peer down through them to the dry rivers and villages standing to their roofs in dust. She knew about the favelas. Teresa's history filled her with pity, curiosity and uneasy guilt. It was not possible, in Rio, to escape poverty, always there, forcing itself on you at every turn of a street, in the shape of children without homes, the street gangs, who slept like abandoned bundles of old clothes on pavements, who swept down on fountains like flocks of birds, chattering and shouting, then drinking like birds with an eye always out for possible police who might lock them up or even kill them.

When Inez knew Teresa had a family in a favela, she asked if she could visit; she had always wanted to go right into a favela but was afraid, and with Teresa she would be protected. At first Teresa said no, afraid that this clever, fastidious friend might despise her, but then she said yes. She had a reason. She told Inez to wear shoes that could not be damaged, and herself put on jeans and a white shirt and flat shoes. The two young women took a taxi to where they could see the favela climbing up the hill, and then toiled up dirty paths through the shanties and shacks to the top, where they found Teresa's father asleep on a bed made of plastic strips tied to a wooden frame found on the rubbish dumps, and the mother sitting under a little porch of sacks stretched on poles, the sick little girl on her lap.

The mother's face did not relent, looking at her daughter, who handed her – without looking at her – an envelope with the money in it. She coldly greeted Inez, though she was impressed, Teresa knew, because no one could ever think of Inez as a prostitute, she was so superior. Her mother did not offer them anything, but Teresa went past the sleeping man to the shelf where water was in a plastic bottle, poured out two glasses for Inez and herself; but then there was nowhere to sit. Teresa could see Inez did not want to drink out of a glass she was bound to think of as contaminated. The two young women stood there, while the mother sat, fanning the sleeping child, and staring down over the higgledy shanty roofs. Then she did relent and asked Inez what she did, and Inez said she worked in a laboratory. The angry woman, determined not to smile, did lay the child down on its bed in a corner, and brought out two stools, gave one to Inez and one to Teresa. She asked where Inez had met Teresa – her voice on *Teresa* was a bitter accusation – and Inez said it was when Teresa was working on a television film. This is what Teresa had wanted to come out of the talk, and now it had: her mother was clearly softened, impressed, and when she looked at Teresa now, though she had been trying not to see this disgraced girl, as if she did not exist, her eyes were full of tears. At the moment of parting she embraced Teresa, which she had not done for a good two years now, and she wept, and so did Teresa, and the mother went on crying as she watched the two clean pretty young women go scrambling down the steep paths to the bottom of the hill.

Inez was affected by the visit. She wept too, sitting with Teresa back in the flat, Ben watching. She said that she admired Teresa so much, oh, she could not bear to think of all those poor people, how clever of Teresa to have survived all that. She was sincere enough, and Teresa knew it, but she was thinking, And I have to thank you for something you'll never understand. For Inez did not know Teresa had been a prostitute; if she had, probably she would have admired Teresa and disliked her own safe life even more.

Now there was a turn of events that would not have surprised Johnston and Rita. Inez worked for a biologist, a friend of her parents, who ran a department of the laboratory. She told him about Ben, describing him as a yeti. 'Something like that, at any rate,' but no one could say what he was. 'He's a throwback,' she said. 'At least, that's what I think. You ought to have a look at him.'

Inez told Teresa that her boss – she put it like that, tactfully, not saying that she had known this 'boss' all her life, as a friend of her parents – would be interested to meet Ben. Teresa was at once on her guard. She was afraid. This immediate, honest and true reaction was swept away because of her awe at words like scientist, science: she knew nothing about all that, her education had not been much more than reading, writing and arithmetic, and a lot of religion. She knew she was ignorant, but not how ignorant: Inez's education was to her a wonder, something distant and unreachable, and she marvelled that Inez knew scientists as colleagues the way she herself knew bar girls and actresses who were more often than not out of work, and singers who were glad to sing in clubs for their suppers and perhaps a few *reais* more. Inez was glamorous because she worked in a laboratory, and understood the secrets of the modern world. Teresa asked what this scientist was going to do with Ben, and Inez replied, 'Just take a look at him.' Inez knew she was being deceitful, but her education had taught her that truth, scientific truth, was more important than anything else: you could say that her education had as much religion in it as Teresa's. She had a pretty good idea that 'having a look' at Ben would not be the end of it, but she felt powerful and useful, introducing this creature who was obviously a kind of scientific enigma, to someone who could solve it. She did not say any of this to Teresa, who knew she was being lied to, and that Inez's cool smiling face was suddenly that of an enemy. Their friendship died at that moment.

Teresa insisted that the meeting must be one that wouldn't frighten Ben, and so it was arranged that next Sunday Inez and her 'boss' and a few more friends, all known to Ben, would assemble. Ben was not told anyone special was coming. Meanwhile Teresa was in a seethe of anxiety, even while she assured herself that the situation could not go out of control: had she not set terms and conditions, had Inez not promised to respect them?

Teresa and her friends, with Ben, were already sitting around the table midday on Sunday when Inez arrived with Luiz Machado, a handsome urbane man of forty or so, smiling to set these people at their ease. He ran a department in the institute which investigated rainforest plants, one of many similar departments, and while something like Ben was not in his line, there was another department, 'the bad place' in fact, run by someone who would find Ben a prize. While Luiz Machado was determined not to be intimidating, it was evident he was not easy in this company. He had criticised Inez for being too friendly with Teresa and for going into the favela: she might have been killed or kidnapped, he said; and if she wanted to get herself a good husband (and he knew she did) then she should be careful: this low life she liked so much might put a discriminating suitor off.

His smiling brown eyes shed benevolence generally around the table, and then focused on Ben, a long, sharp inspection. Ben's eyes seemed to darken as he stared back, and then began to dart about the room. He was making as good an impression as he ever could: Teresa had taken him to have his hair and beard cut, he was wearing a good shirt, one made for him, and he was smiling, the wide scared grin people misunderstood. The scientist reached out his hand to shake Ben's, but Ben grinned.

Luiz sat down, by Inez. Only Teresa knew why Luiz was here: they all knew Inez, at least by name, as a rich girl who gave money to the theatre. Conversation picked up, there was food and wine. Ben sat silent, his eyes on Luiz when they were not apparently looking for ways to escape. As for Luiz, all affability, he did not again inspect Ben as he had at first, but his glances at him were frequent, and each time he took in more information. Ben was not eating. Teresa was afraid he would go next door, and they would hear that thud, thud, thudding. Inez smiled a good deal, and her demeanour when looking at or talking to Teresa was all apology, though she did not know it. This usually so self-possessed, cool young woman was guilt embodied, and Teresa was uncomfortable. It was not an easy occasion. Soon Luiz said he had to return to his lab – yes, there was something he had to check, Sunday or not, experiments did not respect the calendar. He got up, and at his glance Inez, who had been preparing to stay, got up too. The two superior ones went off, in a little fussing of goodbyes and thank yous.

And now people relaxed, and the fun and pleasantness returned to the occasion. But Ben went off to his room, and sat at the window, having put on his dark glasses: the afternoon sun was filling the sky with light, and struck white fire from the wings of seabirds.

When the sounds of the visitors had gone he returned to the

sitting room and found Teresa still at the table, and she was crying. She was in a trap and did not know what to do.

'When can I go home?' said Ben. 'When is Alex taking me home?'

Teresa stopped crying, because Ben had mentioned Alex: usually he did not. Ben must be really frightened.

She did not reply.

'Who is that man?'

'He is a very clever man.'

'What is he going to do with me?'

This acuteness sharpened her forebodings. She acknowledged he was right with, 'I don't know, Ben, but he wouldn't hurt you.'

'I don't like him.'

Teresa didn't like him either. Between her and Inez, in spite of their so different backgrounds, was the instinctive ease women so often feel with each other, but there was nothing like that with Luiz: his affability, the ever-smiling handsome face put all her instincts on the alert.

Next day he telephoned and Teresa said, 'I don't like that, I don't want to do that.' Then Inez was talking to her, and Teresa said, 'No, Inez. I am saying no.' Ben was in the room and so she was inhibited. In the end she agreed that one Alfredo, a friend of Luiz and Inez, would come to talk to her – to her and to Ben.

She put down the receiver and found Ben's wide grin confronting her.

'Ben, they want you to do something. It won't harm you.' Ben's grin remained, and his eyes were roving everywhere. 'It's nothing much. And I'll do the same things, with you.'

'What things?'

'They want to do tests.' She had to explain what she knew about tests, which was not much. 'They want to take some of your blood and find out something.'

'Why I am different from everybody?'

'Yes. That's it, Ben.'

'I don't want to.'

It was lateish that evening when the doorbell rang: this Alfredo had to come from the research station, which was miles away, in the hills. Teresa saw that Ben was trembling, and said, 'It's all right, Ben. Don't be frightened.'

When the door opened, Alfredo was not a superior person but someone like Teresa, a large, brown man, with the same dark eyes and black hair, and as soon as they set eyes on each other they fell into using the accent of the region both had come from. But he had made the dangerous journey ten years ago: he was older than Teresa. He too had arrived in a favela, had got himself out, done many kinds of work, always bettering himself, using his wits and aided by the luck without which nothing can succeed, even for brave and resourceful souls, and ended up as far from his origins as he could ever have imagined possible: he was an assistant in the laboratory. That was what he was called, but in fact he was a general dogsbody. He drove people around, he cleaned equipment, scrubbed work benches, helped prepare samples, and, like Teresa, had learned some English – a good bit more than she had.

Teresa understood at once that sending Alfredo was a brilliant tactic: they were clever people all right. Not only would she, Teresa, be reassured, seeing one of her own people, but Ben could find this friendly fellow easy to like and to trust. Ben sat with them at the table, trying to understand what they were saying – all animation as they spoke of their childhoods, their vicissitudes, their escape from the favela. Because he did not understand, he used his eyes. He knew this man did not mean him harm, and because Teresa liked him so much Ben did too. But at the end of all that talk Teresa said, 'Ben, they want you to go with me and have some tests. But I'll have them too – first me and then you. You'll see that I'm not hurt, and then you won't be worried.'

'I don't want to,' said Ben.

While all the nostalgic chatter had been going on, Alfredo had been observing Ben, and now he said, 'They want to find out about your people.'

'I don't have any people. I'm not like my family – at home. They are all different from me. I've never seen anyone like me.'

'I've seen people like you,' said Alfredo.

Ben's response was such that what Alfredo might have been going to say next simply fled from his tongue. Ben was leaning forward, his eyes all gratitude, tears were rolling down into his beard, and he was pressing those great fists together: he seemed to have been lit from within by fires of joy.

'Like me? People like me?'

'Yes,' said Alfredo, and knew that he should be going on, but could not destroy that happiness there, in front of him. Ben was letting out now short choking sounds, but those tears were not spilling out because of a heavy-weighted heart, but because he was too happy to bear it, and he got up and began a stamping dance around the room, letting out short barking roars which the two observers knew meant that a lifetime's sorrow was being dissolved away.

Meanwhile Teresa was looking enquiringly at Alfredo: she knew there was more he should be saying, but knew too that like her he was awed into silence by what he saw.

'People like me,' Ben was chanting, 'like me, people like Ben.' And he interrupted his dance to ask, 'Just like me?'

'Yes, just like you.'

'Will you take me to them?'

And now, this was the moment when Alfredo should come out with the truth, which would put an end to this joy. He simply could not do it. As for Teresa she was thinking that she had had no idea of the weight of sorrowful oppression on Ben's heart, though she had known he was miserable, had been concerned for him. This exultation, this exaltation, it was a reaction to something she had not been able to imagine. This was because she had never experienced anything like it. She had been unhappy, she had been frightened, but what could he have been feeling all this time?

Ben's dance went on, so noisy that Teresa was worrying about the people downstairs: but perhaps they were out. And then Ben came back to the table, sat down and said to Alfredo, 'Will you take me tomorrow?'

'It's a long way off,' said Alfredo. 'A long way from here. In the mountains, a long way.'

'And first we must go to the place to have tests, you and me,' said Teresa.

'We don't have to,' said Ben.

'Yes,' said Teresa.

'Yes,' said Alfredo.

And as Ben knew that meeting his people at last was dependent on his agreeing to the tests, which had now come to seem to him quite a minor thing to be undergone before Alfredo could take him to the mountains, he agreed to go tomorrow with Alfredo and Teresa: Alfredo would come and fetch them.

He did not sleep, and Teresa lay on her bed, sometimes weeping, sometimes miserable, and thinking too of Alfredo whom she knew was a man for her. He liked her. If this business with Ben had not been there between them, that night she might have spent dreaming of Alfredo. But those tests – she was afraid. All she knew was, they would take blood. She did not like the sound of that, but knew it was done all the time. There would be injections, and she was afraid of those. Modern medicine had passed her by, except for when she had gone to the doctor to be checked for venereal diseases, and that had been an ordeal she never wanted to repeat. Yet Inez spoke of tests and injections as if it had never occurred to her that people might be afraid of them.

And she was thinking, too, of Ben lying awake, too full of joy to sleep.

Before Alfredo had gone off she had managed to whisper, while Ben was out of earshot, 'Did you really see people like Ben?'

'Pictures,' said Alfredo. 'I found them in the mountains when I was working in the mines. Pictures on the rocks – ancient people did them. You know, like the pictures on the rocks at home. Only much better than at home. Not all cracked and broken.'

She understood why Alfredo had not been able to tell Ben the truth. She ought to tell him herself – and could not. That happiness of his, it seemed to fill these rooms, she could feel it surrounding her. She could hear Ben's grunts and sighs and little roars when she got up to go to the kitchen to get herself some water. His joy was so great that it had to escape from him in sounds that made her smile, although she was so nervous about tomorrow.

Next morning Ben was dressed and brushed and ready and sitting at the table looking at the door when Alfredo came. First, there would be a car journey, but he was ready for it.

They drove along the front, Ben averting his eyes from the dazzle off the waves, and then went away from the town and through lush fields where cows grazed up to their middle in grass, towards the hills ahead. Ben sat gripping the edge of the windows, which were down to give him air, but even so he felt sick, and Alfredo stopped the car so Ben could get out. Teresa did too. Ben was sick, and then stood at the edge of the road gazing at the hills: he was thinking of how to run away, but remembered that Alfredo had promised . . . and he got back into the car which was soon going up a twisty hill road. He gripped Teresa's hand, he was feeling so bad, but she said, 'Look, look, Ben,' and he opened his eyes to let out a grunt of fear, because above them three men were floating down under big coloured things like square wings. Ben had never imagined anything like them, and he said, 'What is it, what are they doing?' And Alfredo said it was all right, they were only sky fliers – 'You know, Ben, they are like umbrellas and they carry them down slowly.' The three got out of the car and stood gazing up, up, up, while these sky men floated down past them, aiming for a landing place that was well out of sight down the curving road. Ben's mouth was open, as he stared.

'Could we do that?' he asked.

'Yes, we could,' said Alfredo, understanding very well how not only Ben, but Teresa too, must be feeling oppressed by the rich clever world where people could leap off into air under umbrellas and feel safe, because their lives had always been safe. 'We could if we had the money.'

'Money,' said Ben. 'Where is my money?'

'It's in the safe in the flat,' said Teresa. There wasn't all that much of it left, but Teresa was sure that whatever else Alex did, he would be careful to replace what she had spent.

'Would you like to do that?' asked Alfredo, really curious about how Ben saw these sky men, who were disappearing downhill as they watched.

Ben was silent, staring, and they did not know what he thought.

Back they got into the car, and up they went through hills. Beautiful they were and Teresa thought so, and was grateful to be seeing them, but Ben was sitting with his eyes shut. They had to stop again, so he could be sick.

When they reached what they had heard described as 'the institute', imagining a building, what they saw was something like a town: a lot of low buildings were scattered about, and among them taller imposing buildings, one of which announced itself in large black letters as a hospital. But everywhere over the world is flung a kind of grid or net of hospitals, chemists, laboratories, research institutes, observation stations, and their functions blur and blend. Ben and Teresa were still looking for 'the institute' when the car stopped outside a building in no way different from a dozen others. Alfredo opened the car doors for them. He was looking nervous, apprehensive. This was because he had been ordered on no account to go near a certain group of buildings, nor to tell Ben and Teresa anything about them. What went on in these buildings everyone who worked here was ashamed of, or, if not ashamed, then defensive, even though their work lay in very different areas. By now Alfredo was more than interested in Ben – everyone had to be that – he was sorry for him, and guilty, too, because when he had mentioned those rock pictures, telling Ben he had seen people like him, he had not been thinking, and what he had achieved was something so bad he had not begun to measure it. At some point Ben would have to be told the truth, and disappointment was not the word for what he would feel then. Meanwhile, a nearer worry: what were these people – and Alfredo did not much like his employers – planning for Ben? Their warning not to let Ben know about *the bad place* – or 'The Cages' which is how most people described it – meant that some kind of harm was intended. Alfredo liked nothing about this situation, only Teresa, and when he told her these tests were not so bad, and gave her a smile he meant as reassurance, it said much more. Ben and Teresa were taken inside a large room that had all kinds of apparatus in it, and Alfredo parked the car; he had hoped to return to be near Teresa, but he was given other duties.

In the room were two young women wearing white overalls. One was Inez, who had had to borrow an overall: it had been decided her presence would reassure Ben. He was frightened, and so was Teresa, but she was determined not to show it.

The assistant had been carefully instructed. She asked Ben to 'help' Teresa by sitting close to her and holding her hand while she sat on the edge of a low table, and held out her arm to have a rubber tube put on, and then inflated, and her blood pressure taken. Then it was Ben's turn. He was grinning, which reassured the assistant, who didn't know what that meant, while his blood pressure was taken. He hated the rubber tube tightening around his arm. Then Teresa was told she would have blood removed from her arm. She shut her eyes and averted her face as the syringe filled with dark blood. And now Ben: would he agree?

'Come on, Ben,' said Teresa, 'now you must do it too, like me.'

Ben allowed the needle to go in, and watched as the barrel filled with blood. This scene was not new to him: he had had tests done, when he was a child. He was more used to them, in fact, than Teresa, whose childhood had certainly not included expensive medical care. So far, so good. And now, eye tests. Another woman came in from somewhere to do these. Ben had undergone tests recently with the oculists in Nice, so he did not mind these.

Ears . . . Inez asked Teresa to ask Ben if he had had ear tests, and Teresa said, 'Why not ask him yourself?' Her voice was low and bitter; she was finding herself unable to look at Inez, who was guilty and defiant.

'Have you ever had hearing tests, Ben?' Inez asked.

Ben knew that his hearing was sharper than anybody's, but all he said was, 'Yes.'

He put up with the instruments poking into his ears, and the light being shone in.

And now urine: Inez was expecting him to pee in front of them all – like an animal, Teresa thought – but Ben took the flask and looked about him for cover. 'A screen,' ordered Inez, and to Teresa her voice sounded sharp and scornful. Behind a screen Ben peed, and brought back the flask.

They cut off a bit of his hair, and parings from his nails, and shavings of skin.

All this Ben put up with, silent, stolid – grinning.

Now they wanted to put clamps on his head to measure brain activity, but when Ben saw the apparatus he backed to the door, wanting to escape, and Teresa's encouraging cries (prompted by Inez) that she would do it too, did not persuade Ben.

Inez said, 'Very well, we'll do the x-rays.'

Teresa permitted herself to be x-rayed – for the first time in her life. It was a long process. Legs, arms, feet, pelvis, spine, shoulders, neck. They did not suggest doing the head, so as not to frighten Ben. He stood by, watching, and as the photographs were processed and held out to Teresa and to him, he seemed interested, looking at Teresa's bones.

'Have you ever been x-rayed?' asked Inez.

'Yes,' said Ben. 'I broke my leg once.'

Inez's impatient sigh suggested that he might have told them that before, but all she said was, 'Then you won't mind doing it for us, will you?'

He went through it patiently, Teresa beside him, and Inez on guard.

And now it was getting on in the afternoon.

Ben said, 'I'm hungry.'

They did not want to cause comment by taking him to the canteen. Sandwiches were brought. Teresa was hungry. Ben could never easily eat bread, but he took out the meat fillings and ate them. Teresa asked for fruit, and when it came he eagerly ate it.

Now Inez said he must have the wires attached to his head for brain tests.

'No,' he said. Then he shouted, 'No, no, no, no!'

They had planned to test the workings of his digestive system, his circulation, his breathing: there were a great many more to

133

do, but the tests on his brain were considered the most important, and Ben shouted, 'No!' and began stamping about.

Inez went out to the telephone, her slim compact little body in its white overalls showing a determination that Teresa understood.

'I want to go home,' said Ben, meaning the place in Rio.

Inez came back, smiling brightly and falsely, not looking at Teresa, who knew that deceptions were being planned, and said that Alfredo would take them both back.

The swooping looping drive back down through the hills made Ben sick, and they had to stop twice. At last they were driving along the sea front, and then were in the flat. Alfredo came in long enough to say that they wanted Ben to go back tomorrow for more tests. He knew that Ben was going to say no, and he did.

Alfredo and Teresa stood close together, looking at each other. Their eyes spoke clearly, saying they were going to defend Ben, and that they were angry about what was happening; saying, too, that they liked each other, very much. If Ben had not been there, humped over the table, banging his fists down again and again, probably the two would have been in each other's arms, or at least something would have been said. This strong understanding they had, as if they had known each other always, ended in their marrying, some months in the future. So their story at least has a happy ending: things turned out well for them.

Alfredo went off, and Teresa and Ben sat at the table, and Teresa cooked for him, steak, and more steak, because he was hungry.

She was so anxious she did not sleep much, because she knew bad things were being planned. She could hear Ben moving about his room, but at least he was not banging his head on the wall.

Next morning there was a telephone call: Luiz Machado was coming to discuss Ben. Teresa told Ben this and now she did hear the thudding on the wall. She sat at the table, quite still, for some time, and her breathing was shallow and scared: then she began smoothing her long black hair as if it were life itself she was trying to bring into order, and so she waited, telling herself that now she must be strong, and stand up for Ben – and for herself. It felt to her that even the thought of these powerful people made her want to faint, or to run away; she was being expected to confront what she had held in awe all her life: the educated, clever all-knowing world of modern knowledge. Who expected her to? She, herself. Alfredo. And poor Ben.

Luiz Machado was not alone, for with him came one Stephen, another American, Professor Stephen something or other – she couldn't get the name: Gumlack, or Goonlach – and this one was a tall thin bony man, with a face all big bones, and a big mouth pushed forward by his teeth. His eyes sat inside hollows of bone, prominent eyeballs that seemed to jump out at her when he blinked. He came from some famous institute in the States: she knew it was famous because when he presented the name to her he expected her to recognise it and knew too that because she did not respond she was being classed as an ignoramus.

Ben came into the room, and she understood the two men expected her to dismiss him so they could discuss him and then give her orders. She said to Ben loudly, because she was afraid her voice would shake, 'This is Luiz Machado – you met him, Ben, and this is Professor Stephen . . . Gumlack . . .'

'Gaumlach,' he said promptly, showing he was irritated.

'Professor Gaumlach,' she repeated carefully. 'He comes from America, like Alex.' To them she said, 'Alex brought Ben here to make a film with him.' To Ben she said, 'Sit down, Ben. It's all right.'

The two men were put out, she could see. She was triumphant: she wasn't going to dismiss Ben, as she had been in her time, like a servant.

A brief silence, then Professor Stephen Gaumlach leaned forward, and said, 'This is very important, very important indeed.' His lips mouthed the words, moulding each one as it came out, rolling them towards her like cold marbles. His eyes were cold, fanatic, obsessed. Seldom had she disliked anyone as she disliked this man. 'You must see that, Teresa —'

'My name is Teresa Alves,' she cut in.

This took him aback. He sat blinking. Recovered himself, went on: 'Miss Alves, this is probably the most important discovery of my entire life. You've simply got to understand this. This is a unique opportunity. This . . . Ben, is unique.'

'Ben Lovatt. His name is Ben Lovatt.'

This really did silence him. The big protruding mouth poked forward at her, in annoyance, and he looked for help to Luiz Machado who was listening, detached, calm, urbane.

Ben listened, grinning, glancing about as if in the corners of the room might open an escape route — into woods perhaps where only he knew the turnings, the ways out into safety. He was thinking, But there are people like me, Alfredo told me there are; he would have said this aloud, if he were not so frightened.

Teresa said calmly, 'If Ben agrees, that is all right. If he doesn't, then you must not force him.'

Professor Stephen's orator's mouth opened to object, as he forcefully leaned forward, raising his hand, but Luiz smiled agreeably and said it was not a question of force. This in Portuguese, for her; but in English, for his colleague's benefit, he said, 'He must be made to understand the situation.' Back to Teresa, in Portuguese, 'You do not understand how very important this is. This is Professor Gaumlach's area of research. He is a world authority. This is important for the whole world.'

'You keep saying so,' she said, in Portuguese. Then, aloud, in English, 'But I am in charge of Ben. Alex Beyle left Ben Lovatt in my charge.'

She knew that Luiz at least would know about Alex from Inez; was very much afraid he would also know by now that Alex did not intend to use Ben. It was one thing for Ben to be on the payroll of a film company, even if only in prospect, another if he were some poor derelict, with nowhere to go.

She said aloud, 'Ben must decide for himself.'

Now the two men were looking at each other: they were making silent decisions, she knew.

Suddenly inspired, she said, 'Ben has his own passport.'

She was amazed at herself for not thinking of this before.

The men were brought up short by this announcement: they had certainly not expected it.

She said, 'He is a person of Britain.' She did not know the word citizen. 'You can't make him do anything.'

A short silence: this was because the men's silent colloquy, the decisions agreed to, had not been overthrown by hearing of Ben's legal status. Luiz got up, and so did the American. They said goodbye to her, formally, 'Dona Teresa' from Luiz, 'Miss Alves' from Professor Gaumlach. And they left, not looking at Ben.

Later Alfredo rang to say that things were not good. He had been ordered to drive down to Rio, talk to Ben, and if he refused to go with him back to the institute, he must use force if necessary.

'They can't do that,' said Teresa. 'How can they do that?'

'I said no,' said Alfredo. 'I told them, no. And now I have no job.'

'Then come here if you have nowhere to go,' she said. She was trying to find out if Alfredo was married, or had a woman, had a place to go, and Alfredo said, 'It is lucky I am not in the institute's accommodation. I am living with a friend in his house,' – telling her what he knew she was asking. 'But I will come and see you tomorrow, Teresa.'

When he arrived next morning the door of the flat was open and broken and neither Teresa nor Ben was inside.

What had happened was this. When she and Ben had finished breakfast, both nervy, jumpy, expecting something to happen but not knowing what, Teresa said she had to go out to the shops. She told Ben to stay inside, and not answer the doorbell, unless it was Alfredo. Ben obediently sat himself at the table, and when the doorbell rang shouted, 'Is it Alfredo?' But then there were knocks, many of them, increasingly peremptory and noisy. Ben was silent, knowing that he should not have said anything at all. There was an assault on the door, and two men rushed in, put their arms into his on either side, gagged him while he struggled, and ran him to the lift, and then out of the lift to a car. There they wound up the windows, tied Ben's wrists, his knees, his ankles, and let him thrash about in the back of the car while they drove fast up into the hills. Once they had to stop because Ben had been sick and the gag was choking him with vomit. They took out the gag, poured some cheap wine – the only liquid they had – to clean his mouth, gagged him again, with the same piece of cloth, and at the institute drove at once not to the place he had been in yesterday, but to the 'other' place, which Alfredo had been told not to let him see. It is not difficult to hire people for this kind of work anywhere in the world and in Rio it is certainly not more difficult than in other places.

When Teresa returned with her shopping she found the door open and smashed and Ben gone. This slammed into her diaphragm and she could hardly breathe. She collapsed on to the table, her arms spread out, her head on an arm. Her first thought was, Alfredo is coming, he will help. She did not know he had been and had left and was driving as fast as he could back to the institute to find out what was happening. Then she thought, Perhaps Alex will come. But he had telephoned two days ago to say he was off on another trip to visit the tribe. 'My Indians', he had called them.

It never occurred to her that she might telephone the British Embassy and say that a British citizen had been kidnapped. She did not know a citizen of a country had such rights, knew only that a passport gave you an identity which officials respected. She had often leafed through Alex's passport, with its many visas, thinking: Perhaps one day I'll have one like this. I'll travel to these countries too.

She could not think clearly for a while, and then remembered that Alfredo had not come, so he would telephone her to say why. She was too restless to wait calmly and moved about the room in a blind way, even bumping into a chair. She opened the window wider to let in more of the heavy warm air. Slowly Inez came forward and filled her thoughts. Yes, Inez: she telephoned Inez and when she heard her voice said, 'Listen, it's Teresa . . .' And then, fast and decisive, 'Don't go away from the telephone, Inez, don't do that.' She heard Inez breathing, and knew she was afraid. 'Where is Ben?' she demanded. 'They took him away. So where is he?'

She heard a feeble, 'I don't know,' and said in a cold voice that surprised her, 'You know. You know. Is he where we were before?'

'No,' said Inez. There was a silence, during which both could hear the other's breathing. And then Teresa said, 'I will kill you. If you don't help me I will kill you.' And now Inez understood what it was that had attracted her about this representative of the hard wild life of the poor, why she had courted Teresa. The thrill of fear she felt at those words ran through her body and even hurt her eyes. She trembled, listening to Teresa. 'You were my friend, my friend, Inez. And you did this.'

'I didn't know,' Inez managed to get out. 'I didn't know they planned to do this.'

'But you know now, Inez. You know where he is.'

Inez did know because she had seen the car that had Ben in it driving past. Everyone in the institute had known. People crowded at windows and heard stifled roars and bellows from the car. Some claimed they had seen Ben heaving and struggling. Inez knew – they all did – where they were taking Ben and she felt sick. She was not the only one. The laboratory assistant who had tested Ben was shocked. What she told the others had percolated through the institute. This yeti, this freak, was a polite sort of creature, almost like ordinary people: he should not be treated like this. What was happening was that the unease, the shame, most felt about what went on in the 'other' buildings, was being crystallised around this Ben, who – they soon all knew – had been kidnapped.

Now Inez heard Teresa say, 'You must come and fetch me. I must find Ben. I must come to where he is.'

'I can't,' said Inez. 'I can't just leave my work.' But she knew what she would hear next: 'Inez, I mean what I am telling you. I will kill you. I will know that you are a bad person.' And Teresa went on to order her to come into Rio, pick her up, and do it now. 'Ben has a passport, Inez. They can't do this. You tell them.'

Inez was in the laboratory during this conversation. The assistant from yesterday listened, and said angrily to Inez, 'Why are they doing this? He is not an animal.'

Inez went out to her car, unobserved, so she believed, by the senior staff – by Luiz – and drove down to Rio, thinking that she might lose her job. She did not really believe she would. What was happening – it was illegal. She was pretty sure that the plan was to get this Ben – she had no feeling for him, did not even think of him as a person – away from the institute at some point, and then he would disappear. People disappeared. Luiz – no, not Luiz, that American – was counting on something, and she believed he was right: everyone in the institute would be so frightened of losing their job, their precious hard-to-come-by jobs, that they would keep quiet. As for herself, what crime was she committing? She was leaving her office in the institute for a couple of hours. She drove fast and found Teresa waiting. She had a holdall with some clothes for Ben and his dark glasses.

She did not know what she was going to do when she – when they – found Ben. Just before Inez arrived Alfredo had telephoned to say that he had heard from the driver at the institute who was replacing him that Ben had been taken to the bad place. Alfredo told Teresa to come to where he was, a room in a house not far from the institute, in a village. They would decide how to rescue Ben together.

The drive up into the hills was a silent one. Teresa watched Inez's profile, kept towards her, cold, pure, hostile – and guilty. She was afraid of a trap: did Inez plan to kidnap her too? To stop her helping Ben? Suddenly – she had not known she was going to come out with it – Teresa asked Inez just this, and Inez began to cry, and said that she, Teresa, was unjust and cruel – Inez had not kidnapped Ben, had she?

When they reached where Alfredo had said she must be set down, Inez stopped the car, and heard Teresa say, as she got out, 'Tell them they have done a wrong thing. It's wrong. The police could punish them. You tell them.'

Inez had no intention of saying anything, hoping only that her absence had not been noted.

Teresa stood in rutted dust on the edge of a track, the sun beating down on her, and saw Alfredo coming from a little house. Their smiles at each other spoke from a dimension far from their anxieties over Ben, and he put his arm around her as he walked her to his room.

It was now afternoon, about three o'clock. Alfredo knew where Ben was and told Teresa about it. He said they should go there as soon as it was properly dark. At night there was no one at The Cages – but there might be tonight, because of Ben. He was drugged, the other driver had said. He had heard Luiz and the American talking, in the car. Luiz was in two minds about what was happening: it was the word 'passport' that had reached him. Stephen was determined to keep hold of Ben. 'He's a bit mad, that one,' said this man, Antonio, Alfredo's friend. 'He's like a dog with a bone. He's got it and he's going to keep it.' Antonio knew The Cages better than Alfredo did. He said a good pair of wire-cutters would be needed, and the first thing must be to cut the wire of the alarm, which went to the main office building where there was a guard all night. And after that, what did Alfredo intend to do? Alfredo told him. Antonio then said he himself must be included in any plan for getting away because he would certainly lose his so recently acquired job.

Plans were what Teresa and Alfredo now discussed. If they could get Ben right away from Rio they believed pursuit would not follow. Alfredo told Teresa that if there was a pursuit then the British representatives in Rio must be alerted. Teresa listened with interest while she heard how citizens in foreign countries might be protected from local harm. She had never imagined such a degree of concern by a government for a little person, such as herself. But they were up against a madman, the American professor. She was not surprised to hear that Antonio had said he was mad: she had thought he was. She could easily see again that big protruding mouth, pushing out words at her while the green eyes stared unseeing, for the man's attention was all inwards, on his obsession.

'Is it important?' she asked Alfredo. 'Is it important to know what Ben is?'

'They say he must be a throwback to – a long time ago. A

long time. Thousands of years. They can find out from him what those old people were like.'

The idea did attract Teresa, but it was in a different part of her from her passionate concern for Ben. She thought that she felt towards him like she would a child – something helpless, at any rate. She did not care about those old people. She loved poor Ben.

During that talk, in the hot bare room, drinking Coca-Cola, they reminded each other that there was an immediate and shocking problem. Ben believed that Alfredo knew where Ben's people were.

'We've got to tell him,' said Teresa, remembering Ben's delight, and how his whole being seemed to enlarge and thrill with his thoughts about them. Even as she spoke she felt herself cringe away from telling him. To say it was all an illusion, only pictures on a rock wall . . . cruel, terrible. But he had to know.

'Can we take him to see the rock pictures? That would be better than nothing, don't you think so?'

'When I was working in the mines near Jujuy I went into the mountains – high up, Teresa. I like that, being by myself in the mountains. But these are high, high, high, not like ours at home. Not many people go up there. One morning I woke up – it was dark when I went to sleep – and there right in front of me were pictures on the rock. The sun was shining on to them. When the sun is shining you can see them well, but when the rock face is in shadow you can walk right past and not see them . . . But we've got to get there.'

Teresa knew how much money Ben had left. She had a good bit put away, but she wasn't going to use one *real* more of that than she had to. Alfredo had savings. There was more than enough for three cheap flights. 'No problem,' said Alfredo. 'I'll tell my friend to come and fetch us in his car. I have friends. I worked in the mines for three years. I'll get work again. I'll keep clear of Rio for a little. I had to do it before – I'll tell you, Teresa.'

Both were thinking that if he stayed to work in the mines and Teresa stayed with him then everything she had built up in Rio would go for nothing. Would there be theatre, dancing groups, film-makers, in Jujuy? she asked. Alfredo's answer was, 'I earn good money in the mines. And they know me. I could stay a year and you could wait for me in Rio.' This was the first time their understanding was put into words. 'We can marry in Jujuy, so we can be sure – and a year goes quickly.' Teresa was looking back on the three years she had been in Rio, so packed with events and people, and they seemed very long to her. 'We can talk later,' he said quickly, seeing her doubting face.

It was getting dark. Up a hill, through trees, they could see the lights of the institute. They took wire-cutters and walked quietly as if they were off to visit the living-quarters of the institute, where most of the employees lived, but went past there, and into the forest that surrounded the institute. Neither of these children of wild places feared anything in the forest. They padded quickly along a path their feet seemed to know was there, passed the main buildings of the institute, leaving them behind, and then, ahead, a few hundred yards, lights burned on a separate group of buildings. From them came yelps, calls, cries. This was a bad place: Teresa knew it, and Alfredo whispered, 'I don't like coming here.'

Where was Ben? They stood at the edge of the trees, looking at the scattered buildings and did not know where to go. Then

Teresa heard it, a low intermittent rattling, bang, bang, bang, and a rattle again. 'There he is,' said Teresa, 'he's there,' and she began running across the space of flat dust to the building. As they ran, the sound grew louder, the rattling bang. It was dark now. The light on this building was at the front, and they stole around to the back and saw windows. They were open. A foul smell came out. First Alfredo and then Teresa scrambled up over the sill. A low light was burning on the ceiling. In tiers of cages were monkeys, small and large, arranged so that the excrement from the top cages must fall down on the animals below. A bank of rabbits, immobilised at the neck, had chemicals dripping into their eyes. A big mongrel dog, which had been carved open from the shoulder to the hip bone and then clumsily sewn up again, was lying moaning on dirty straw, its backside clogged with excrement. (This dog had been cut open six months before and from time to time the wound was unpicked to see what its organs were doing, it was subjected to this drug or that, and then sewn up again like a hessian sack. The edges of the wound were in fact partly healed, in crusts, and through them could be glimpsed the palpitating organs.) From cages monkeys stretched out their hands and their human eyes begged for help. Teresa saw nothing of all this. She was looking at Ben, kneeling on the floor of his cage, bang-banging his head on the wire. He had not been drugged: Professor Stephen wanted him uncontaminated. He was unclothed, this creature who had been clothed since he was born. In the corner of his cage was a pile of dung.

'The alarm,' Teresa said to Alfredo, who began looking around for the wire, and at her voice Ben sat up and howled, his face lifted towards her. 'Be quiet, Ben,' whispered Teresa. 'We're going to take you away.' His eyes – what was wrong with them? In the feeble light they seemed like dark holes, but they were blanked out with terror and misery. 'Ben, Ben, be quiet, you must be quiet.' He quietened but his breathing was like groaning. Alfredo had found the wire for the alarm and had cut it. Then he vomited: the smell, that smell – and it was so hot in here.

He began cutting a big hole in the wire of Ben's cage, which was for a strong animal – thick wire. Teresa was looking at a cage where a white cat was lying stretched out, a mother cat. Wires led into her head from an instrument fastened to the wire of the cage. Four kittens sucked at her: each had wires on its head. The cat looked at Teresa and the accusation in its eyes made her want to put her hands over her own eyes. There was a big hole in Ben's cage. 'Quiet, quiet, be quiet, Ben,' whispered Teresa, and put her arms around him to hold him. He was filthy and shivering, a poor helpless defeated creature who now – surprising them – made a leap out of her arms and out of the window and into the dark. He was running for the forest, and Teresa and Alfredo ran after him. 'Stop, Ben! There are people, don't go further, come here.' She and Alfredo moved cautiously about under the trees, in the dark, and could hear nothing. Yet she knew Ben was there. 'I'm going to sit down here, Ben. And Alfredo too. He's a friend. Come here to me. And we'll take you to Alfredo's house and then we'll go right away.'

A silence. Little forest noises. Behind, in the building they had left, monkeys set up a howl, a terrible sound, from that hell which is multiplied all over the world, everywhere human beings make our civilisation.

'Ben, Ben, come here to me, Ben.'

It was the smell that told them he was coming.

'Will you take me to the people who are like me?' they heard.

'Yes, yes, Ben, we will,' said Teresa, desperate with his desperation.

He was there, by them, crouching, trembling.

'Now, come quietly, quietly, Ben. Don't make a sound, Ben.'

It was all right in the forest, they were well hidden, but they had to cross a bare space, taking the risk of being seen. Luckily most people were inside eating their evening meal. They could hear television sets, radios, voices. Alfredo said, 'Now, run.' And Teresa, 'Run fast, Ben.' The three ran, through the dark cut by lights falling from the houses, to Alfredo's room.

There Teresa pushed Ben into the shower, washed him, ran water until it was lapping clear around his feet, pulled him out, dried him, put on the clean clothes she had brought. Alfredo found orange juice for him, and fruit. He wanted to drink, but not to eat. His eyes were on Teresa, imploring her: like those monkeys' eyes, she thought, though she had not taken them in at the time.

'Why are they allowed to do that?' she asked Alfredo.

He was silent, and grim, and – she could see – ashamed, and said, 'It's science.'

Ben was not trembling now, but he found it hard to look at them, and sat crouching on his chair, fists dangling, head poked forward, eyes still painful with fear.

'We are going to drive you down to Rio,' said Teresa. 'Then tomorrow we are going on an aeroplane.'

'To my people?'

'Yes,' she said, helplessly, and did not dare even to look at Alfredo. What were they going to do?

About midnight, when the houses of the institute's workers were dark, and nothing seemed to be moving, they crept out, listening to a dog bark, and found Antonio waiting for them in his car. The four drove down to the city. It was late in the night when they reached the flat. The door had had slats nailed across it, presumably by the janitor.

They told Ben to go to bed and try to sleep. He was not to be afraid. Meanwhile Alfredo, Teresa and Antonio conferred. Antonio had worked in the mines too. He produced his identity card, laid it on the table and said to Alfredo, 'Is yours OK?'

Alfredo brought his out from an inside pocket, and put it down beside Antonio's. Teresa could see that there had been problems of some kind with these cards, but that now things were in order. They were looking at her, and now she took her card from her handbag and the three documents lay together on the table. She was thinking of Alex's passport, and found these three sheets of inferior paper, the identity cards, insulting.

'One day I want a real passport,' she said to Alfredo. Antonio laughed in surprise, but Alfredo, having begun to laugh, stopped, seeing from her face she was saying something of importance. 'I want a passport like a little book, like the foreigners have – like the Americans.' Alfredo nodded, and waited for her to go on. She dismissed her identity card with a gesture of contempt. 'It's not good enough,' she said.

Alfredo pondered this, then said, 'All right, I'll make you one now.' And he got up, found some paper in a drawer, folded it into a little book, brought it to the table, and sat down, looking sternly at Teresa, a biro poised. She was already laughing and Antonio was too.

'Both crazy,' said Antonio. 'Loco.'

'Name?' demanded Alfredo, like an official.

'Teresa Alves.'

'Dona Teresa Alves. Your hair is black?'

Later, through their lives, they would relive this scene, reminding each other, and telling their children, how Alfredo had found out first about Teresa, her life, about her – while Antonio sat smiling and nodding and Ben slept next door.

'Dark brown,' said Teresa, and held a lock forward for him to see.

'Black in the shade and brown in the sun,' said Alfredo. 'I've noticed. I'll put black.' He wrote it and then: 'Your eyes are black, I'd say, but *they* aren't going to look into them. Shall I put black?'

'That will do.'

'You are – how tall?'

She told him.

'Nearly as tall as me. A good height. Do you have any distinguishing marks? They always want to know that.'

'I have a small mole on my – lower back.'

Antonio laughed.

'On your bum?'

'Yes, and another on my shoulder here,' and she held her collar away from her neck and he peered at it.

'I think we will keep these moles to ourselves,' he said. 'Anything else?'

'I've got this scar where I fell chopping pumpkins for the goats,

I fell on a sharp stone.' She held out her arm: a thin white line ran down her wrist to the top of her palm.

'They don't need to know,' said Alfredo. 'Right, then. Height, hair colour, eye colour – that's enough for them. What's the name of your village?'

'The same as yours. Dust village, dust province, dust country. But it was Aljeco.'

'We'll put that. Your birth date?'

She hesitated, uncertain whether she wanted him to know how much younger she was than she had said.

He saw her reluctance and said, 'I'll put the same as mine. Now we'll need a photograph.'

And now he handed the little package of folded paper to Teresa with a bow. 'Your passport, Dona Teresa.' And she got up from her chair, took the thing from him, and curtsied to him.

They passed the time, chatting, and Antonio said he would follow them to Jujuy, and to the mines. He would be happier out of Rio for a bit. When the light came they drank coffee and the two men went off to arrange flights.

Teresa went in to Ben, found him awake, and said he must be brave and patient. If anyone came to the flat, she would be sure they would not come near him. She was going to lock him in, and this must not frighten him. She said all this because she was pretty sure 'they' would come after Ben, and with the door broken there was no way to keep them out. She took him juice, said it would be best if he slept, and on no account to make a sound if anyone came.

It was not long before she heard the men outside. She opened the door saying, 'Do you see what your thieves did to this door?'

– putting them in the wrong, though they looked, she thought, like policemen chasing a criminal. 'Sit down, please,' she said, and sat herself, noting that both were staring at Ben's door.

Luiz sat at the head of the table, taking the commanding place from force of habit. The American was opposite Teresa, the protuberant cold eyes prepared for anger.

Teresa began at once: 'That was a bad thing you did. You stole him from here. He is not your property.' She was speaking to Luiz, but he said, 'I am not to blame. I had nothing to do with it. That part of the institute has nothing to do with Brazil: it is under separate international control.' And he waited for Stephen Gaumlach to speak. He did not: he had twisted himself to stare at Ben's door.

'But you are both here,' said Teresa, seizing the – to her – nub of the situation.

'I am an old friend of Professor Gaumlach's,' said Luiz.

'But you knew those men were coming to get Ben.'

'I am apologising – on Professor Gaumlach's behalf,' again directing his colleague with a look. It was ignored. 'Instructions were exceeded. The door should not have been broken in.'

'If you expected us just to give Ben to you then why did you send criminals? They were just street criminals.' And before either man could say anything – the American seemed to feel no need to – 'And you put Ben into a cage like an animal, without clothes.'

'I've told you,' Luiz Machado said. 'That had nothing to do with our institute. But it was obviously a misunderstanding.'

Teresa said, 'I think the misunderstanding was that you did not expect us to find him like that.'

Here Luiz nodded, acknowledging that she was right, and

that, too, he was impressed by how she was standing up for herself: she knew – must know from Inez – how important he was.

Now Stephen Gaumlach spoke, as if he had heard nothing of their argument. 'You can't keep him. You don't understand, do you?'

'I know you want him for your experiments. I know. I've seen with my eyes . . .' And she indicated her eyes with her two forefingers.

He leaned across the table to her, fists clenched, his face dark with rage. 'This . . . specimen could answer questions, important questions, important for science – world science. He could change what we know of the human story.'

And now Teresa felt attacked direct, into her great respect, her reverence, for knowledge and for education; that area, like a window into an unknown sky, where she could have bowed down and worshipped – and she burst into tears. She told herself, furious, that she was tired and that was why she was crying, but she knew the truth. As for Luiz, he believed this ignorant girl was frightened because she was challenging authority, and was going to get into bad trouble because of it. Knowing Professor Gaumlach as he did – he did not much like him – he saw Teresa rather as he might a mouse that has decided to stand up on its hindlegs and threaten a cat.

As for the professor, he was irritated that Teresa was crying.

Both men thought she was defeated: there was a great deal she could have said in accusation that she had not – laws had been broken in ways that could easily have serious consequences. But it was not calculations of a legal sort that made her say what she did now. It was the hateful bullying face in front of her, those cold angry eyes, while in her mind's eye she saw Ben howling naked in the cage, she saw the white cat, with faeces dripping down on her fur from the cage above. She said in Portuguese, '*Voce e gente ruim.*' The hatred in her voice did reach her antagonist, if he did not understand her words. Now she said in English, 'You are bad people. You are a bad person.'

She did not address this to Luiz, and this was not because he had absolved his institute from all blame, nor in her mind were thoughts of a political kind – this American was a member of the most powerful nation in the world, that kind of thing: she was not interested in politics. No, she disliked Stephen, she hated him, as instinctively as she judged Alex Beyle a kindly but weak man who was good to her while he was around but forgot her the minute he left. She knew that for this famous professor to insert wires into a cat's head, and her kittens' heads, and measure her feelings as she tried to feed them while dirt dripped on to her white fur, to make monkeys sick – she could see now only too clearly the little paws stretched out to her for help – he would do anything at all and never think of what it cost the animals. He was a monster of cruelty.

But she was still weeping because of the conflict that was tearing her apart.

Luiz said, 'You say that Ben is owned by – what did you say his name was?'

'Inez – she's your friend, isn't she? – she must know the name. Alex Beyle. He's an American film-maker and Ben will be the star.'

'I understood that there will be no film?'

'That isn't certain. Alex is in . . .' She named the little hill village where Alex and Paulo were working on their script, or scripts, knowing that it was not likely Luiz would know it. 'He is off on location now. The weather is bad. The telephone is not good. I shall tell him what has happened when he telephones me, and I'll say you want to talk to him about Ben.'

Her voice was steady now. She got up. 'If you'll excuse me, I have work to do.'

Slowly, the two men got up. Luiz, as always, was calm, was smiling. As for the other man, staring at Ben's door, he looked like a red ant – she knew now what the resemblance was that had been bothering her to recognise it.

She said, 'Ben is asleep. He is not well after what was done to him.' And she stood in front of Ben's door.

'You must not take Ben out of the country,' said Stephen, threatening, seeming to loom over her.

'He can go where he wants. He has a passport,' she said.

Luiz said to Stephen, 'We should go.' His voice told both Stephen and Teresa that there was a plan in his mind.

The two men left. Teresa wept, from relief; she was shaking all over because of what the confrontation had cost her. She knew that these men – she did not distinguish between them, saying this one is responsible, that one is not; they both had power, and were alike, for her – would do something soon to make possession of Ben legal. This time it would not be a kidnap: they would have the law behind them: Ben would be arrested on suspicion of something or other.

Teresa used the interval before Alfredo and Antonio returned to pack clothes for Ben, going quietly in and out of his room so as not to wake him – he was moaning in his sleep. She put in a warm jersey and a cap, and did the same for herself.

When Alfredo and Antonio came back they heard from her what had happened, and knew they should hurry.

'Quick, Ben, we're going on an aeroplane, far from here,' Teresa said, while he sat up in his bed, frightened, and then all eagerness. 'To my people? Now?'

'Come on, Ben,' said Alfredo. The look Teresa and Alfredo exchanged confessed their helplessness: how could they put an end to this eager hopefulness? Yet they must, they would have to.

Teresa left a letter on the table for Alex, saying that she and a good friend were taking Ben to a safe place – she was careful not to say where, because she knew it would not be Alex who would read that letter first. She had told the janitor to report the break-in to the police, and to board the door up more securely.

And so they left Alex's place, and in the street got into Antonio's car: he would take them to the airport. There he said goodbye, but he would see them soon in Humahuaca, which was where Alfredo would find work; it was a couple of hours' drive from Jujuy.

This was a big aeroplane, of the kind people use to go from continent to continent, but at São Paulo they changed to a smaller one, with very different people in it who had a look of being engaged with the work of the world. This plane flew lower, bringing the landscape up towards them, and its shadow flitted about over rough terrain where people like Teresa were walking and looking up to see an aeroplane, in which none of them could hope to travel, pass overhead. But once Teresa had thought she would never be in an aeroplane. Ben was looking down, and with interest. Apart from that first little hop over London with Johnston this was the first time he had been awake on a plane and ready to notice what was around him. At first he found it hard when Teresa said, 'Look, that's a big river down there,' or, 'That's a range of hills.' He asked, 'A river? That's a river?' Or, 'Those are hills? They look flat.' Then his mind adjusted and he took it all in and was pleased and proud that he was understanding. But that little grin of his, not the wide scared one, told Teresa and Alfredo what he was thinking about.

'Are we going to find my people today?'

'No, not today, Ben, they're away in the mountains.'

'Those mountains down there?'

'No, those are small mountains compared with the big ones. You'll see for yourself.'

The plane descended in Paraguay, and people got on and off, and then what they saw beneath them were green-and-yellow plains, and cattle, and soon they would be in Humahuaca. Antonio and Alfredo between them had decided that it would be much better to arrive there, with the miners and engineers and other workers for the mines, than in Jujuy, where they might look at travel documents more seriously. As the plane came down it could be seen that a lot of people were drifting along below them towards the mines. No one made a fuss here about frontiers, or how people crossed them: thousands of people – who could say how many? – traversed frontiers which in their minds were no more than imaginary divisions.

At the little airport building Teresa was prepared to bring forth her identity paper, but the man at the desk recognised Alfredo:

he had once worked in the mines himself. Alfredo said Teresa was his sister. The official did give Ben another look, but waved through this big bulky man who in this crowd did not seem so remarkable.

Meanwhile the plane they had come on departed for the short hop to Jujuy: on it were mostly workers bound for the tobacco plantations there. Alfredo had telephoned a friend to ask him to come with his car to Humahuaca, to meet them. He had not arrived yet. They sat on chairs under a tree, glad of the shade. It was stingingly hot. Teresa said she had a headache, the altitude was getting to her. Ben said he felt fine: he did not seem able to take in the concept of altitude, until Alfredo pointed to the Andes, and said that Ben must imagine the sea at the foot of the mountains, and then imagine himself climbing up, counting with each step.

'Is that where we are going to find my people?'

'Yes, it is.'

Ben sat smiling, making the rough little sounds that were a song, if you knew him.

They were watching people coming past them, to the mines.

'Mines need workers,' said Alfredo. 'And they don't ask questions.'

'And what questions could they ask you?' she asked, feeling she was on the edge of a precipice. 'What are you afraid of in the airport in Jujuy?'

'When they took me on at the institute they asked where I had worked. I said Jujuy. I didn't say Humahuaca: never tell them more than you have to. So if they wanted to get me into trouble over getting Ben out of The Cages, and driving him down to Rio, then they would have telephoned Jujuy. But I think they won't bother with that, I am sure they have worse plans in their mind for Ben.'

They were talking in Portuguese, and Ben heard his name and said, 'What are you saying?'

'Only that we took you away from that place.'

Alfredo went on, in Portuguese, using the local accent they shared, which was almost impossible for an outsider to understand, as if afraid of someone overhearing – though there was no one within earshot. 'But there's something else, Teresa. When I came here to the mines it was because I was in trouble. That was seven years ago. But they keep records – the police have my name from that time.'

And he told her a story she felt she had heard so often she could have taken the words from him and gone on herself.

Getting out of the favela had been as difficult for him as for her. He had been in a street gang, committed petty crimes, and the police knew him. One night there had been a fight between him and the gang leader – a knife fight. The boy had not been killed, but he was hurt quite badly, and he blamed Alfredo, though it was he who started the fight.

Alfredo decided to remove himself from Rio. Three years later, with money saved and skills learned in the mines, he returned. The street gang he had been part of had gone – disappeared, and the boy whom he had wounded was dead, because of another fight. Alfredo was a man now, full of responsibility and competence: he had got work easily, and ended up at the institute.

Now this was where Teresa should tell him about herself, and it was so hard for her, her voice got lower, and stumbled, and was inaudible. She had to tell this man, whom she knew she loved, that she had been a whore. Alfredo was embarrassed. He shifted about as he sat, even seemed about to get up and walk away. 'Teresa, you tell me another time. You tell me when you want to.'

'But I must tell you. I have to tell you.'

'Listen, Teresa, you forget, I came to the favelas, just like you. I know about . . . I have a sister there still. She hasn't got out yet. Later I will help her.' He leaned forward, smiling, though she knew it was not easy for him, and took her hand. 'We will help her together, Teresa.'

'Are you talking about me?' Ben asked again.

'No, about us,' said Teresa, in English.

Now Alfredo's friend, José, arrived with his car, and they drove the ninety kilometres to Jujuy. The two sat in the front, talking, and Teresa was with Ben in the back. She knew he would feel sick: it was an old rattly car.

The mountains rose up on their right, and they were in their shadow.

'Are we going tomorrow?' Ben asked.

'No. We have to arrange things to take with us.'

'When are we going?'

'Perhaps the day after.'

She was trying to make herself say, 'Look, Ben, you don't understand, we haven't explained it well . . .' But she could not get it out. What are we going to do? she was asking herself. How are we going to tell him?

José had been with Alfredo working in Humahuaca. When Alfredo left, and Antonio, he took a course in mining engineering, which lifted him out of the rut of common miners. He had a little house in Jujuy. He had a wife, who worked there. Most weekends he came home to her. She was not there now: she was visiting relatives.

It was a neat little house, with three rooms, and a kitchen, and a shower. There was television and radio. It was like the house Alfredo had been sharing near the institute: it was like houses for people of their kind all over the world.

They ate their supper, with the television on, but no one was watching it. Ben was in his dream, and the men were talking, and Teresa watching and listening. She was pleased Alfredo had this good friend — had two good friends, because this made her feel supported herself. A man with good male friends — she knew the value of that, for a wife. Her father had had his friends, in that time that seemed long ago, in their village, but since coming south, no friends, only his wife. In the favela, no men to sit around with, and talk. He drank, alone. He got drunk.

Teresa knew that since she had met Alfredo half the weight and worry of her life had been lifted off her. Already, so soon after knowing him she found it hard to imagine what it had been like, alone, with only herself to depend on.

When it came to the time of going to their rooms then there could be no doubt that Alfredo would be with José, and not only because they had not finished exchanging news. Now, if she had been alone in the house with Alfredo — but he lifted his hand to her, with a smile, as a *goodnight* and went with José. It was she who had to be with Ben because he trusted her. She was thinking that in Alex's place Ben had his own room, but now there were two beds, within touching distance. She put on a nightshirt, in the shower room, and found Ben lying dressed on his bed when she returned. She knew it was because in his imagination he was already beginning the journey into the mountains. He was smiling up at the ceiling, and he asked, 'Will we start early?'

'Not tomorrow, Ben. I told you.'

She turned out the light at the door and went into her bed, thinking that since she had known Ben he had been most of the time sick, frightened, cowed, and she had not seen him as he really was, happy and confident. Even in the half dark of the room she could see that face of his, and he was smiling. This was the moment when she should say, 'Look, Ben, there's been a mistake . . .' But moments, then minutes, passed and she was silent.

I'll talk it over with Alfredo and with José too, and we'll work out how to explain it to him; but what nonsense was this, she was thinking. Ben expected to meet his own kind, and he was not going to let the dream go. If they said, 'But Ben, better if you didn't see them, they are poor wretched people,' – he would want to meet them. If they pretended to find a place in the mountains where the people had been, and then said, 'They seem to have moved away somewhere,' Ben would go on searching, for his need was so great. Teresa tried to imagine what it was like, believing yourself to be the only person in the world like yourself, knowing you are alone, dependent on chance kindnesses, used but then abandoned – but she couldn't imagine it, only a panic of emptiness and aloneness that gripped her, making her cold and sick. *But we have to tell him, we have to*, she was repeating to herself, as she fell asleep, and woke to see Ben standing over her. Outside was a strong yellow moonlight and the room was light enough. Ben had his jacket and trousers off, and what she saw there, in his hand, made her sit up and say sharply, 'No, Ben, no, stop.'

He was bending over her, and she did not know if he intended only to look at her, or . . . He straightened, his hand dropping away from a shrinking penis.

'You should go back to bed, Ben,' she said.

He did so, silent, obedient, and lay awake. So did she. He said angrily, 'Rita liked me. She liked me. You don't like me.'

'Yes, I do, Ben. You know I do.'

She heard his breathing: it was rather like a child's who is about to burst into tears. She thought that this . . . man, whatever he was – strong and full of energy when he wasn't miserable – had his instincts; and what had he been doing for sex, for women? Rita was a long time ago – months. She knew that as he lay there, snuffling a little, he was thinking that when he met his people there would be a woman for him. Soon his breathing changed, and he was asleep. She did not sleep. As soon as the light came she was up and dressed and went to the kitchen to make coffee. The smell of it woke the men.

The door between this room and Ben's was closed but even so she was speaking in a low voice, telling them that they must explain things to Ben, they must, it was cruel to go on like this.

'He will find out,' said Alfredo. 'He will see for himself.'

'I am afraid,' said Teresa, but did not mean for herself, or for them, but first Alfredo and then José assured her that they would all be together and if Ben was angry they would defend her, and themselves. Alfredo saw she was not reassured and said to José that Teresa was fond of Ben. 'And I am too. He's not just a – beast.'

'He feels things the way we do,' said Teresa.

And here Ben came in, smiling, as eager for the new day as a child, and before he could ask, 'Can we leave today?' she told him that today was for doing the shopping.

They all went together in José's car to buy more warm things for the mountains, plastic cans for water, a blanket each, food. That took all morning.

Then Teresa complained again of her headache: the altitude was making her feel sick.

José brewed coca tea and made them all drink it, for the altitude sickness. She slept away the afternoon, while the men went off to see someone, and Ben fidgeted about in the sitting room.

At supper Alfredo and José told Teresa they had a plan for her. She could stay here in this house, with José's wife, who worked in Jujuy and kept her weekends free for when José came from Humahuaca. That morning they had been to see a friend who worked in the local television station – a small one, nothing like the splendid provisions of Rio, and if she was patient there would certainly be something for her. Meanwhile, there was the archaeological museum, she could try there. Jujuy attracted tobacco men, mining men, experts of all kinds, and they needed people like Teresa to look after them. What did she think? Would she stay in Jujuy? asked Alfredo, and she answered at once, yes. Ben was listening to this conversation as a child does when the talk does not concern him, but Teresa thought, and for the first time, What are we going to do with Ben? If we send him back to Alex, that Professor Gaumlach will get him. I can't ask José's wife to take in Ben, too. They had scarcely thought of Ben's future: it had been so urgent to get him out of Rio, out of danger. It rather looked as if she – and that meant Alfredo (but why should he say yes to it?) – was now responsible for Ben. Or perhaps he should be sent back to London, to this Rita Ben talked about.

'What time will we go tomorrow?' asked Ben.

'When we've got all the things into the car,' said José.

'Are we taking them to the people?'

'No, we need them,' said José. 'It will be cold.'

'Why do they live in a cold place?'

'You'll see,' said Alfredo, after a pause, when the three pairs of eyes met, and separated again at once, in case Ben should see their anxiety. But he had seen: oh, yes. Ben understood very much more than ever people knew.

'Why did you say it like that?' he wanted to know. 'Is there something wrong with them?'

'No,' said Teresa, and José came in with the reminder that it was not yet eight o'clock, and why not all four visit a certain hotel, and see for themselves the night life of Jujuy?

Ben said he did not want to: Teresa said that he had liked sitting on the pavements in Rio and watching life going on, hadn't he?

The hotel was a gimcrack place, far removed from the stately edifices along the famous beaches of Rio. There were coloured lights on its outside, isolating it from the rest of the area, and in the main room it was bright, crammed, noisy. The entrance of the four was hardly noticed, and as for Ben, the place was full of strong bulky men. Food was arriving at the tables, but the bar that filled a wall was what people came for. All along the bar stood men, mostly from the tobacco estates, eyeing the bold loud young women who were there for them. The four found a table and squeezed themselves in; Ben did not look happy: the noise was affecting him. It was upsetting Teresa too, in her present state, with headache and nausea only just held at bay. And she was watching the girls and assuring herself that she had never been so pushy and noisy, she was sure of it; telling herself that they, like herself, probably had families to support – and wishing she had never come. Then she saw a young woman she had last seen at a café table outside the first hotel she had used, in her new dress. She was afraid she would be recognised and greeted and that José would know about her. That wouldn't be nice for Alfredo. She shrank back behind Alfredo, who noticed it, looked to see why, understood, and said to her that they need not stay long. Meanwhile José had been accosted at the bar by a girl he obviously knew very well: they were exchanging pleasantries.

'How long has José been married?' asked Teresa, and as Alfredo laughed, she said, 'If I had to wait for you in Rio I'd be jealous.'

She thought Ben wouldn't understand, but he said, 'Why, Teresa? Why are you jealous of Alfredo?'

'We were joking,' said Teresa, watching José with the woman. Then, in a low voice to Alfredo, 'No, I wasn't joking.'

'But you'll keep me out of trouble,' said Alfredo.

At this point José came back with beer for him and Alfredo, juice for Ben, and coca tea for Teresa. 'Tomorrow will be difficult,' he said to her. 'We will be going much higher, and you'll feel bad if you don't drink this tea.'

'Do my people drink this tea?' asked Ben.

'Judging by you they won't have to,' said José. 'Where did you get those lungs?' Then he laughed, in a knowing conspiratorial way, and said, 'I said that as if they existed.' He said it in Portuguese, sharing the cruel joke with Teresa and Alfredo. In

Portuguese: but Ben had caught it, caught something. 'Why are you laughing?' he said to José. He was all at once full of suspicion.

'We make bad jokes,' said José, in English, and then in Portuguese: 'This Ben is quick off the mark.'

'Why did you say that? Why did you say my name, Ben, what are you saying about me?'

'It's nothing,' said Teresa, thinking that this José was not sensitive to people's feelings, not like Alfredo. Then she thought, But Ben shouldn't be finding out the truth like this, in this unkind way.

'What is it?' demanded Ben, looking into their faces, one after another.

And now this was the moment when she could say, 'Ben, there's been a misunderstanding . . .' But she could not make herself do it. She kept quiet. Alfredo looked uncomfortable, seemed apologetic – towards her, she noted, as if this awkwardness had been hurtful for her, not Ben. José returned to the bar to say something to the woman – an acquaintance, or more – Teresa reassured herself that José was not Alfredo.

Alfredo said to José that they should leave. He knew Teresa did not like the place. José would not have noticed. Meanwhile, poor Ben was sitting there morose, looking around with suspicious eyes as if not only the three of them but everyone had become his enemy. Teresa walked by the girl from Rio feeling that her past had put out a tentacle and was pulling her back into it. As the two walked to the car, Ben coming along behind, watching them suspiciously, Alfredo put an arm around her and said, 'But you'll stay with me, Teresa? You agree? And when we come down from the mountains we will get married.' He had said this in Portuguese, and now said in English, for Ben, 'Teresa and I are going to be married.'

Ben did not respond. And Teresa was thinking, How about Ben? Alfredo won't want me if he thinks I must look after Ben.

When they got to José's house Ben said he wanted to go to bed, and Teresa, afraid of what he might be feeling, joined him and lay there in the dark. Ben was not asleep. She could see the restless gleam of his eyes. He did not speak.

She was listening to the men talking next door, seeing them in her mind's eye. They were very different. José was a lean taut man, with a sharp-boned face, and wary eyes. He was pale-skinned under the sunburn, not an even coppery brown, like herself and Alfredo. She was thinking, Our children will be good-looking. They will take after Alfredo and me. We are nice-looking people. José is ugly and it is because he didn't get enough to eat at one time in his life. She knew this was so by a certain unfinished look to him. At least we ate, Alfredo and me, we ate well, before the bad droughts began. And our children will be healthy. She was imagining Alfredo's face, when he saw their first child. While these confident and self-respecting thoughts went on, her heart was beating with anxiety about Ben.

In the morning Ben was silent and did not ask questions. While the car was being packed he stood staring at the mountains, and in between these long sombre stares, turned to look at them, his eyes puzzled, on guard. He began a stamping angry dance, letting out short roars of rage, and this went on until the car-packing was finished and the house was being locked. Then he stopped and stood staring up at those peaks, those cruel, tall, dark peaks. What she saw on his face made her go to him and put her hand on his arm, delicately, for fear of his anger. But he was not responsive to her sympathetic hand: he did not move, only stared, his eyes darkened by pain and by loss.

Teresa was thinking, Then he knows. He must know. Somehow he has understood it all.

In the car Teresa sat in the front, because of fear of feeling sick, knowing that Ben might be sick too: Alfredo was with Ben, and Teresa saw from how he sat that he was ready to reckon with Ben, if his anger broke out again.

The road they were on was at first wide, with townships along it, and the odd hotel, and then became narrower and began to climb. The air was thin and sparkling and Teresa ceased to care about anything but sickness and the altitude headache that crashed in and out of her head in cold waves. The road twisted up the sides of hills and then down again, for these were foothills, and there were still trees, which became fewer, and there were no longer pits of shadow across the road. They were above the tree-line. It was colder, and they stopped the car to put on jackets over their jerseys. Ben stood by the car and stared up, up, and then around, at the hills and peaks and rocky valleys where there was no one, and not a house anywhere. Late in the afternoon they reached the hotel, the last, on that road, which after here became a rough track. The hotel was used by prospectors, climbers, surveyors. They were the only people there. Teresa cared about nothing except that the movement had stopped, and she could sit with her eyes shut. Ben was silent. He stood by windows one after another and looked up. Alfredo went to order the right sort of meal – a light one because of the altitude sickness. And again arrived a tray with coca tea, which they all thankfully drank. They were over the 16,000-feet mark, and the only one who was not feeling the strain was Ben.

'It's that chest of yours,' said José. 'In this region everyone has a chest like yours, because the air is thin and you need big lungs.'

'Who, everyone? Where are they?' asked Ben. 'There isn't anyone.'

It was a cold night, with cloud drifting past the windows: nothing to be seen. They went to bed early, José with Alfredo, Teresa with Ben. Teresa was awake, because of her headache, and Ben was awake. It was dark and stuffy in the room but the whiteness of the mist outside, lit by the lamp that hung over the entrance, sent a thin pallor into their room. Teresa was thinking that if she told Ben now, that his own kind, his people, did not exist, it would be no more than what was in his mind.

They were up early, in a thin exhilarating thrilling air, the sun striking hard off the rock faces and the peaks. There was not a sign of mist, or of cloud. As they ate their breakfast, two men arrived; they planned to take off into the peaks, but return before it was dark. 'Not a place to get lost in, when it's dark,' they said.

And now, reorganisation of gear, of belongings. They retained one room and put into it all they would not need, because from now on they would use their feet. And the car was locked and left where the proprietors of the hotel could keep an eye on it. Each had a backpack, filled with warm things, water, food; and José had a little stove, and a pan.

They were not going higher but keeping roughly on the same

level. At least, José added cautiously, with an eye on Ben, not for today. The news that today would not see the end of their journey was received by Ben in silence: not easy to read his face, as he stared at the immensities around. What she believed she saw there made tears fill Teresa's eyes and she turned away. Before setting off, the four watched the two new arrivals walk off, up, into a steep crag that was keeping the hotel in shade.

That night they expected to find a hut, used by climbers, and tomorrow morning they would look for the rock face Alfredo remembered. Now they all had on their thickest jerseys and padded jackets, and all wore dark glasses. At first they were on a track, wide enough for a donkey, or a mule, but then there were paths, sometimes in shade, sometimes in sun. Alfredo kept stopping as paths diverged to make sure of the route: he and José argued about it. José said that they should choose the better-used paths, 'because that is where the rock men go'. Meaning the archaeologists, the palaeontologists, who discovered things in the mountains that filled the museum down in Jujuy. He asked Alfredo why his particular rock face (he called it 'your picture gallery') had not been discovered.

'You'll see for yourself,' said Alfredo.

They said this in front of Ben in English, but he did not ask questions, only followed José, who followed Alfredo. Teresa came behind, where she could watch Ben. She was pretty sure Ben knew the truth, but then on to that bearded face appeared a look of such longing, such wonder, that she felt it was a child she was looking at, who was expecting tomorrow's promised marvels, and then that look disappeared and she saw only sadness.

It was a hard day for them, though they were not climbing

much higher. Sometimes they moved along paths in deep shadow between tall crags, sometimes they walked along the edges of precipices. Their chests hurt – though, it seemed, not Ben's – and they had headaches, in spite of José's potions of coca tea, which he dispensed from vacuum flasks. They stopped in mid-afternoon, because there was a hut, not more than a rough shelter made of logs, which must have been brought up here on beasts, because there were no trees. Alfredo said he remembered the hut, which had been in a better condition then: there were gaps in the logs where they had settled and some slates on the roof had slipped. No one had used it for a long time, only some small animal, who had left droppings. They made the place clean, and stacked their things around the wall. José collected bits of twig and lichen for a fire, but there was so little of this material it was decided to save it till dark. The night fell early, because of the tall peaks all about, but there was time for Alfredo to establish the route for tomorrow: he clambered about among the rocks, stopping at an implacable rock face or on the edge of a precipice. As the cold struck, and the sun dropped out of sight, they were inside, with their blankets arranged around the little fire. Their heads were ringing with the height, and no one wanted to eat much. The other three were waiting, their nerves on the alert, for Ben's, 'Where are my people? Where will we find them?'

Alfredo had a tiny radio, but it was not working well. A faint tinny music jigged from somewhere thousands of feet below; voices, male and female, faded in with fragments of news, a phrase from a song, words of a speech – they switched it off.

The fire was tiny, a mere flicker on the log walls. Through the chinks in the logs could be seen a cold light. Out they went, and all stood transfixed. No pollution in these mountains and the stars were a cold coruscating brilliance, flashing fires of blue, red, yellow, pressing down towards them, and the Milky Way was flung across the sky like a road to somewhere. Seeing those stars thus, clean and clear and unconcealed, was like revisiting a memory. They were silent, struck into awe, and then from Ben they heard a rough tuneless singing, and saw that he had begun to move – he was dancing and singing to the stars.

'They're talking!' he shouted. 'They're singing to us.'

Trying to open their minds to what Ben could hear, the three seemed to hear a high crystalline whispering, a tiny clashing, but Ben was exulting, 'The stars are singing, they are singing!'

He danced on, bending and bowing and stretching up his arms to the stars, stamping and kicking up his feet, and whirling about and around, on and on, while the watchers shivered and held themselves in their blankets.

And on he went; and on, till they thought he would fall down from exhaustion, there, outside the little hut built between the rocks and the crags whose tops pierced the field of stars.

It seemed to them that hours were passing, while they were shivering themselves into insensibility, and first Teresa, then the men, retreated into the hut for warmth, from where they saw Ben moving about in the starlight through the chinks and heard his hymn to the heavens.

Later he was quiet, and they went out and saw him standing with his arms outstretched and his head back, silent, looking up, and up. The crackling brilliance overhead had moved its patterns, and star shadows had reached across the bare space to where Ben stood. He was in a trance, or an ecstasy, and then at last he let

173

his arms fall, and stood still and began to shiver. Teresa brought him inside, and put blankets around him. He sat where she had arranged him, staring into the remnants of the fire, and he began his low rough singing again. He was far from them, and from consciousness of them. They spoke in low voices not to rouse him from this state he was in. They did not sleep, but kept a vigil, with him.

In the morning, when they opened the door, the hut was still in shadow, while the sky spread gold and pink among the peaks.

They warmed themselves with hot tea, and walked about outside the hut to get the stiffness out of them. Not Ben, he was lost in his dream, whatever it was: they did not know. They left everything in the hut, and walked off in single file on a narrow path with a tall black cliff on one side, and on the other a slope of black rock down to a rocky valley far below them. Above them floated a condor marking their progress along the slippery path. After a couple of hours Alfredo said, 'It's here. I remember it.' He struck off sharp to the right through a crack in the cliff, where they had to creep and clamber and support themselves on tiny ledges and protuberances, and then they emerged into a big flat space, with crags towering all around, and, in front of them, a tall rock face. It was now about ten in the morning. The sunlight was on the other side of the barrier of rock they had come through, and above there was a bright sunlit sky. Alfredo was moving about, along the base of the rock face, stood nearer . . . moved back . . . went forward again, shook his head . . . shifted to this side, and then to the other, saying, 'No, not here, yes, it's here,' – went off, came back, and suddenly a shaft of light came weakly over a peak, but immediately strengthened, and reached the rock face at its edge.

At once a figure stood out from the black shining depths of the rock, where, deeply immersed in the shine, were other figures, that needed the sunlight to bring them forth. The shaft of light became a flood and there they all were, a gallery of pictures, Ben's people. He had taken a step forward, then another, stood in front of the rock, as the three stayed behind him, letting him take possession. Now the sun was hard and full on the rock face, and it was crammed with pictures, at least forty of them, and several were like Ben, except for what they wore. Were those strips of bark? Skins? They were real clothes, of supple stuff that fell in folds, and were belted at their middles and held on their shoulders by metal clasps. The clothes were coloured, not merely grey and brown, but reddish, blue, green. The hair of these people fell to their shoulders, longer than Ben's now, and they were big-chested. They had beards, but not all, no those must be the females, the ones without beards; and they were smaller, and more delicately built, though they stood solidly on their feet. They were not carrying weapons, though several held what seemed to be some kind of musical instrument. Ben stared. What he was thinking now the others did not know, but their hearts were beating, certainly not only from the altitude, but from fear of what he might be feeling. Ben stood forward, and stroked the outline of a female who seemed to be smiling at him. Then he bent forward and nuzzled at her, rubbing his beard over her, and letting out short cries that were greetings.

The silence then was dreadful, dreadful. Their breathing, harsh and laboured, emphasised it.

Ben's back was still turned to the others. And there he stood stroking that other, who smiled back at him from the depths of the black rock. And now the sunlight was thinning, slipping and sliding across the rock, and as it did, one after another the people disappeared. Soon, only a few were left, on the very edge, and Ben stood touching, stroking, the female creature. Then the sun left her and they heard his howl, as he flung himself against the rock and crouched there.

The sun had lifted itself away from the scene. The pictures had gone. Past Ben's crouching figure they could see, if they stared hard enough into the shiny rock, the faintest outlines of what had been so strong and alive a short time before. Easy to see how people could walk past that rock face and see nothing – nothing unless they were lucky enough to catch just that right moment when the sun fell at a certain angle.

Ben straightened himself, his back still to them: he was taking his time turning to face them. He had been betrayed so dreadfully by these three who called themselves his friends – so he must feel; and they were afraid of what they would see. But he didn't turn, seemed to hang there by the rock face, one fist resting on it. Then he did turn himself about, with an effort: they could see it was hard for him. He seemed smaller than he had been, a poor beast. His eyes did not accuse them: he was not looking at them.

Teresa dared to go to him and put her arm about him, but he did not feel it, or know she was there. He stumbled along beside her on the long walk back to the hut. On the path that had the precipice below it he did stop a moment and look down, but went on at a touch from Teresa. In the hut they put more fuel on the little fire and made tea and offered him some. He did not see them. Then – and it was so sudden they at first could not move – he left them and went bounding back along the path they had just come from. A silence. Then Teresa understood, and was about to run after him, but Alfredo put his arm around her and said, 'Teresa, leave him.'

They heard a cry, and a slide of small stones, and silence.

They slowly got up, slowly followed him. They made their way to where the precipice fell away from the path. There was Ben, far below, a pile of coloured clothing. His yellow hair was like a tuft of mountain grass.

The three teetered there on the edge, peering over, their arms stretched out to hold on to each other, for balance. A gust of wind blew from an edge of blue air where the path turned a corner, just ahead, strong enough to make them move back on this path which was not much more than a ledge over space, to stand with their backs to the rock. Now they could not see Ben, only the other side of the valley, rising up into cliffs and crags.

Alfredo said, 'When we get back to the telephone at the hotel, we can ring Professor Gaumlach and tell him what has happened.'

'I shall ring,' said José. 'He won't know who I am. I won't mention you or Teresa.'

'He will be angry with you,' said Alfredo. 'You can tell him that even an animal has the right to commit suicide.'

'It will take them a day or two to get around into the valley – they will need mules,' said José.

Alfredo said, 'The condors won't leave much of him.'

And there was a condor. It appeared from over the mountain behind them, and floated down past them, and circled over the valley. They could see the sun shining on its back.

177

'Never mind,' said José. 'They can know about a whole person from just a little bit of finger bone.'

'They will want to know what he was doing up here,' said Alfredo.

'Are you going to show them the rock pictures?' asked José.

'Let them find the pictures for themselves,' said Alfredo.

Another condor was dropping from the mountain peaks across the valley.

Teresa had not contributed to this discussion.

José said, 'Teresa, you are silly to cry. It's a good thing, what Ben did.'

Alfredo said, 'But Teresa knows that.'

'Yes,' said Teresa. And added, 'And I know we are pleased that he is dead and we don't have to think about him.'